When she was 16 years old, **Melissa P.** began writing a diary recording her secret desires. That diary eventually became this novel, her debut. A worldwide sensation, it has been translated into twenty-five languages and adapted into a feature film.

ONE HUNDRED STROKES OF THE BRUSH BEFORE BED

Melissa P.

A complete catalogue record for this book can be obtained from the
British Library on request

The right of Melissa P. to be identified as the author of this work has
been asserted by her in accordance with the Copyright, Designs and
Patents Act 1988

Copyright © 2003 by Fazi Editore
Translation copyright © 2004 by Lawrence Venuti

First published as *Cento colpi di spazzola prima di andare a dormire* in
2003 by Fazi Editore

First published in this translation in the UK in 2004 by Serpent's Tail
First published in this edition in the UK in 2012 by Serpent's Tail
an imprint of Profile Books Ltd
3A Exmouth House
Pine Street
London EC1R 0JH
www.serpentstail.com

ISBN 978 1 84668 936 9
eISBN 978 1 84765 573 8

Printed by the CPI Group (UK) Ltd, Croydon, CR0 4YY

10 9 8 7 6 5 4 3 2 1

To Anna

The translator would like to thank Melissa P., for her patient answers to queries about stylistic matters; Lauren Wein, for her help with sartorial terms; and Martha Tennent, for her steadfast support, moral and otherwise.

6 July 2000
3:25 pm

Diary,

    I'm writing in my shadowy room plastered with Gustav Klimt prints and posters of Marlene Dietrich. As she levels her languid, haughty gaze at me, I scribble across a white page that reflects the sunlight seeping through the chinks in the blinds.

    It's hot, a dry, torrid heat. I hear the sound of the TV in the next room, and my sister's tiny voice reaches me as she harmonizes with the theme song of some cartoon. Outside a cricket screeches like there's no tomorrow, but inside a soft peacefulness has descended on the house. Everything seems safely enclosed in a bell jar of the most delicate glass, and the heat weighs down every movement. But inside *me* there's no peace. It's as if a mouse were gnawing away at my soul, so gently that it even seems sweet. I'm not ill, but I'm not quite well; what's worrying is that "I'm not". Still, I know how to find myself: all I need do is lift my eyes and fix them on the reflection in the mirror, and a soft, peaceful happiness will possess me.

    I admire myself before the mirror, and I'm transported by the figure gradually emerging there, by the muscles that have assumed a firmer, more defined shape, by the breasts that are now noticeable beneath pullovers and bob gently at every step.

Ever since I was little, my mother has innocently wandered around the house nude, so I've grown accustomed to observing the female body, and a woman's figure is no mystery to me. Still, an impenetrable forest of hair hides the Secret and conceals it from sight. Often, with my image reflected in the mirror, I slip my finger inside, and as I look into my eyes, I'm filled with a feeling of love and admiration for myself. The pleasure of observing me is so intense and powerful that it immediately turns physical, starting with a twitch and ending with an unusual warmth and a shudder, which lasts a few moments. Then the embarrassment comes. Unlike Alessandra, I never fantasize when I touch myself. A while ago she confided to me that she too touches herself, and she said when she does it she likes to imagine she's being possessed by a man, hard, violently, as if she were going to be hurt. Gosh, I thought, and here I get excited simply by looking in the mirror. She asked me if I also touched myself, and my answer was no. I absolutely don't want to destroy this pillowed world I've constructed, a world of my own, whose only inhabitants are my body and the mirror. Answering yes would have been a betrayal.

The only thing that really makes me feel good is the image I behold and love; everything else is make-believe.
My friendships are fake, born by chance and raised in mediocrity, utterly superficial. The kisses I timidly bestow on boys at my school are fake: as soon as I press my lips on theirs, I feel a kind of repulsion – and I bolt whenever I feel their clumsy tongues slipping into my mouth. This house is fake, so far removed from my current state of mind. I want every picture to be suddenly torn from the walls, a freezing, glacial cold to penetrate the windows, the howling of dogs to replace the crickets' song.

I want love, Diary. I want to feel my heart melt, want to see my icy stalactites shatter and plunge into a river of passion and beauty.

8 July 2000
8:30 pm

A commotion on the street. Laughter fills the stifling summer air. I imagine the eyes of my peers before they leave their homes: bright, animated, yearning for a fun night out. They'll spend it on the beach singing songs accompanied by a guitar. Some will wander off to spots cloaked in darkness to whisper infinite words into each other's ears. Others will swim tomorrow in a sea warmed by the dim morning sun, guardian of a maritime life that is yet unknown. They will live and learn how to lead their lives. OK, I'm breathing too, biologically I'm on track. But I'm afraid. I'm afraid of leaving the house and facing strange looks. I know, I live in perennial conflict with myself: there are days when hanging out with the others helps me, and I feel an urgent need for them. But there are also days when the only thing that satisfies me is to be alone, completely alone. Then I listlessly drive my cat from the bed, stretch out on my back, and think. I might even play some CDs, almost always classical music. I perk up with the music's help and don't need anything else.

But that racket outside is tearing me to pieces: I know that tonight they'll live more deeply than me. I shall remain inside this room, listening to the sounds of life, listening till sleep welcomes me into his embrace.

10 July 2000
10:30 am

You know what I think? I think starting a diary was the worst possible idea. I know what I'm about, I understand myself. In a few days I'll forget the key somewhere, or maybe I'll just decide to stop writing, jealous of my thoughts. Or maybe (this isn't so implausible) my snoopy mother will pore over the pages, and then I'll feel stupid and break off my tale.

I really don't know if it's such a good thing to unburden myself. At least I'm distracted.

13 July
morning

Diary,

I'm happy! Yesterday I went to a party with Alessandra, who looked very tall and thin on her spike heels, beautiful as ever, and as ever slightly rude in the way she talked and acted. But she was affectionate and sweet too. At first I didn't want to go, partly because parties bore me and partly because yesterday the heat was so stifling it stopped me from doing anything. But then she begged me to go with her, so I went along. We travelled by scooter and sang till we reached the suburb in the hills, now transformed by the scorching summer from green and lush to parched and shrivelled. The town of Nicolosi had gathered in the piazza for a huge festival, and the asphalt, cooled by the evening, was covered with booths selling candy and dried fruit. The little villa stood at the end of a narrow, unlit road. When we arrived at the gate, Alessandra started waving her hands and shouting, "Daniele, Daniele!"

He walked up very slowly and greeted her. He seemed rather handsome, though I couldn't make out much in the darkness. Alessandra introduced us, and he gave me a limp handshake. He murmured his name very softly, and I smiled, thinking he might be shy. At one point I distinctly saw a gleam in the darkness: his teeth were so white, so amazingly bright. I squeezed his hand harder and said "Melissa" a little too loudly. Maybe he didn't notice my teeth weren't as white as his, but maybe he saw my eyes brighten and shine. Once we had gone inside, I noticed that in the light he seemed even more handsome. I walked behind him and saw the muscles ripple on his back with each step. At five foot two I felt very short beside him; I also felt ugly.

When we finally sat down on the armchairs in the living room, he was facing me, slowly sipping his beer and staring straight into my eyes. I was embarrassed by the spots on my forehead and by my complexion, which seemed much too fair compared to his.

His straight, well-shaped nose looked just like the ones on Greek statues, and the veins that stood out on his hands endowed them with an awesome strength. His huge dark blue eyes cast a proud, haughty gaze at me. He asked me a stream of questions while displaying utter indifference. Instead of discouraging me, it made me bolder.

He doesn't like to dance, nor do I. So we stayed by ourselves while the others got loose, drank, and joked.

A hush suddenly fell upon us, and I wanted to fix it.

"Beautiful house, isn't it?" I said, feigning self-confidence.

He just shrugged his shoulders. I didn't want to be pushy, so I remained silent.

The moment for intimate questions had arrived. When everybody was busy dancing, he moved even closer to my chair and started looking at me with a smile. I was surprised and charmed, expecting him to make some sort of move; we were alone, in the dark, and now quite favourably close to each other. It was then that he asked me, "Are you a virgin?"

I turned crimson and felt a lump in my throat as a thousand pins pricked my brain.

I answered a timid yes, which immediately made me turn away my eyes in order to quell my immense embarrassment. He bit his lip to repress a laugh and confined himself to a cough without uttering a single syllable. Inside me the reproaches were loud and harsh. "He'll never pay attention to you again! Idiot!" But in the end what could I say? The truth is that I'm a virgin. I've never been touched by anyone but myself, and I'm proud of it. Still, the curiosity is there and it's very strong, particularly a curiosity about the nude male body. I've always been prevented from getting to know it: when a nude scene comes on the TV, my father grabs the remote control and changes the channel. And when, just this summer, I stayed out all night with a boy from Firenze who was on holiday here, I didn't dare put my hand on the same place where he had already put his.

Then there's the desire to experience a pleasure produced by someone other than me, to feel his skin against mine. Finally there's the privilege of being the first among girls my age to have a sexual relationship. Why did he ask me that question? I haven't even thought about what my first time will be like, and I'll probably never think about it. I want only to live it and, if I can, cherish a memory that forever remains beautiful, a memory that will keep me company at the saddest moments in my life. I'm thinking Daniele could be it – or so various things have led me to feel.

Last night we exchanged phone numbers and during the night, while I was sleeping, he sent me a text message. I read it this morning: "It was great to be with you, you're very pretty, and I want to see you again. Come to my house tomorrow and we'll go for a swim."

7:10 pm

I'm perplexed and upset. The outcome I'd been unable to anticipate till a few hours ago was rather harsh, even if not entirely disgusting.

His vacation home is very beautiful, surrounded by a verdant garden and myriads of the freshest, most colourful flowers. The sun's reflection shone in the blue swimming pool, and the water was so inviting you could just dive in. But today, of all days, I couldn't: my period stopped me. Under the weeping willow I watched the others diving and playing while I sat at a little bamboo table holding a glass of iced tea. Every so often he would glance in my direction and smile, and I would cheer up again. Then I saw him climb up the ladder and come toward me, the water slowly trickling down his glistening torso. He swept back his soaking hair and sprayed droplets all around.

"I'm sorry you can't have any fun," he said with a slightly ironic tone.

"No problem," I answered. "I'll just get some sun."

Without a word he took me by the hand as he grabbed the cold glass and set it down on the table.

"Where are we going?" I asked, laughing but a little worried.

He didn't answer. Instead he led me to a door at the top of a stair, lifted the mat, picked up a set of keys, and inserted one into the lock, watching me with a keen, crafty look as he did it.

"Where are you taking me?" I asked again with the same concealed worry as before.

Once more no answer, just a faint laugh. He opened the door, pulled me inside, and closed it behind me. The room was extremely hot and dimly lit by the glimmers that filtered through the shutters. He leaned me against the door and kissed me passionately, making me savour his lips, which tasted like strawberries and were nearly the same in colour. His hands were planted on the door, and the muscles on his back were taut. I could feel them hard beneath my hands while I caressed his back, running my fingers up and down just as the demons were running up and down my body. Then he took my face in his hands, broke away from my mouth, and asked me softly, "Would you like to do it?"

I bit my lip and answered no, because a thousand fears suddenly invaded me, faceless, abstract fears. The hands he had placed on my cheeks exerted more pressure, and with a force

he may have wanted – in vain – to translate into gentleness, he
pushed me farther down, abruptly showing me the Unknown.
I now had it before my eyes, it smelled male, and every vein
that crossed it expressed such power that I felt duty-bound to
reckon with it. It entered my lips presumptuously, washing
away the strawberry taste that still impregnated them.

Then all of a sudden there was another surprise: my mouth
filled with a hot, sour liquid, thick and plentiful. My sudden
start at this new discovery gave him a slight twinge; he grabbed
my head and pushed it toward him even more forcefully. I
heard him panting, and there was a moment when I thought
the warmth of his breath reached all the way down to me. I
drank the liquid because I didn't know what else to do with it;
my throat emitted a soft gurgle that embarrassed me. While I
was still on my knees, I saw his hands drop. Thinking he wanted
me to raise my face, I smiled. But he just pulled up his bathing
suit, and I heard the noise of the elastic against his sweat-soaked
skin. I then stood up on my own and looked him in the eyes,
searching for some reassuring sign that might brighten me up.

"Do you want something to drink?" he asked.

Still tasting the sour liquid, I answered yes, a glass of water.
He left and returned a few seconds later with a glass in his
hand. I was still leaning against the door, looking curiously
around the room after he had switched on the light. I observed
the silk curtains and the sculptures, as well as the various books
and magazines scattered across the elegant sofas. An enormous
aquarium projected its sparkling light on the walls. I heard
noises coming from the kitchen. I felt neither worry nor
shame, just a strange contentment. Only later did shame assail
me, as he handed me the glass indifferently and I asked, "Is this
really the way it's done?"

"Of course," he answered with a derisive smile that displayed
his beautiful teeth. Then I smiled and hugged him. While I was
smelling the nape of his neck, I felt his hands behind me
grasping the handle and opening the door.

"Let's meet tomorrow," he said, and after a kiss that was sweet for me, I went down to the others.

Alessandra looked at me and laughed. I flashed a smile that immediately disappeared as I lowered my head: my eyes filled with tears.

29 July 2000

Diary,

I've been going with Daniele for more than two weeks, and already I feel very close to him. It's true that his behaviour towards me is somewhat rude, and never does a compliment or a kind word issue from his mouth: only indifference, insults, irritating laughter. And yet the way he acts makes me even more tenacious. I'm certain the passion I feel can make him all mine, and he'll soon recognize it. During the hot, monotonous afternoons, I often find myself thinking of his taste, the freshness of his strawberry mouth, his muscles firm and rippling like massive fish. And almost always I touch myself, experiencing awesome orgasms, intense and brimming with fantasies. My passion is overwhelming, I feel it beating against my skin, wanting to get out, to unleash all its potency. I have a crazed desire to make love, I'd do it right now, I'd keep at it for days on end, till my passion is completely out, finally free. I know intuitively I shall never be sated anyway; after a short while I shall reabsorb what I have dissipated only to surrender it anew, in a never-ending cycle, always the same, always exciting.

1 August 2000

He told me I'm not capable of doing it, I'm not passionate enough. He said it with his usual mocking smile, and I left in tears, humiliated by his response. We were lying on the hammock in the garden, his head resting on my legs as I gently caressed his hair and gazed at his eyelashes, quite thick for an eighteen-year-old's. I ran a finger across his lips, wetting the tip a little. He awoke and shot me an inquiring look.

"I want to make love, Daniele," I blurted out. My cheeks were flaming.

He laughed so loudly he lost his breath.

"Give me a break, babe – what is it you want to do? You're not even capable of sucking me off!"

I looked at him, perplexed, humiliated, I wanted to sink into his well-manicured garden and rot beneath it while his feet trod on me for eternity. I fled, screaming "Asshole" and violently slamming the gate. I started the scooter and took off, my soul in ruins, my pride crushed.

Is it so hard, Diary, to let yourself be loved? I didn't think it was necessary to drink his potion in order to secure his affection; I thought I had to yield myself completely to him, but now that I'm about to do it, now that I desire it, he mocks me and drives me away. What can I do? Might as well forget about revealing my love to him. I can still prove I'm capable of doing what he doesn't expect. I'm very stubborn; I'll get my way.

3 December 2000
10:50 pm

Today's my birthday, my fifteenth. Outside it's cold, and this morning it rained hard. Some relatives came over, but I wasn't very hospitable, and my embarrassed parents told me off when the others left.

The problem is that my parents see only what they like to see. When I'm bubbly, they share my delight and seem amiable and understanding. When I'm sad, they stay at arm's length and avoid me like the plague. My mother says I'm a zombie, I listen to funeral music, and the only thing that amuses me is to shut myself up in my room and read books (she doesn't actually say this, but I can read it in her look). My father knows zilch about how my days unfold, and I haven't the slightest desire to tell him anything about them.

Love is what I'm missing, an affectionate caress is what I want, a sincere look is what I desire.

School was also hellish today: twice I was caught unprepared (I've lost the desire to study) and I had to put up with the Latin lesson. Daniele torments my brain day and night and even inhabits my dreams. I can't reveal to anyone what I feel for him, they wouldn't understand, I'm certain.

During the lesson the classroom was silent and dark because a lightbulb burned out. I left Hannibal crossing the Alps and the well-trained geese in the Campidoglio waiting for him. I turned my gaze toward the steamed-up windows and saw my opaque, hazy image: without love a man is nothing, Diary, nothing at all (nor am I a woman).

25 January 2001

Today he turns nineteen. As soon as I awoke, I grabbed my mobile, and the beep-beep of the buttons resounded in my room. I sent him a happy birthday message. I know he won't respond with thanks; maybe it'll give him a chuckle. He won't be able to restrain himself when he reads the last sentence I wrote: "I love you, and that's the only thing that matters."

4 March 2001
7:30 am

So much time has passed since I last wrote, but nearly nothing has changed. During these months I dragged my feet, burdened by my sense of the world's inadequacy. Around me I see only mediocrity, and the mere idea of going out makes me feel ill. Where would I go? With whom?

Meanwhile my feelings for Daniele have intensified, and now I feel like I'm bursting with the desire to make him mine.

We haven't seen each other since the morning I left his

house in tears. Only last night did his phone call break the monotony that has dogged me ever since. I'm hoping with all my might that he hasn't changed, that he's stayed exactly the same as that morning when I made my acquaintance with the Unknown.

Hearing his voice awakened me from a long, sound sleep. He asked me how I was getting along, what I'd done during these months; then with a laugh he asked if my tits had grown, and I answered yes, even though it isn't really true. After running out of words to fit the occasion, I had told him the same thing I told him that morning – I wanted to do it. Over the past few months the lust has been agonizing. I've touched myself till I thought I'd go out of my mind, experiencing thousands of orgasms. Desire took possession of me even during school hours when, certain that no one was watching, I straddled the iron support of the desk and leaned my Secret against it with a gentle pressure.

It was strange he hadn't mocked me yesterday; in fact, he remained silent while I confided my longing to him. He said there wasn't anything weird about it, it was normal for me to have such desires.

"As a matter of fact," he said, "since I've known you for a while, I can help you realize them."

I sighed and shook my head. "In eight months a girl can change; she can come to understand certain things she didn't before. Daniele, why don't you tell me the truth, that you don't have any cunts available, so all of a sudden (and finally, I thought!) you remembered me?" I was letting everything out.

"You disappeared! Do you want me to hang up? There's no use talking to a girl like you."

Afraid he would once again slam the door in my face, I yielded, uttered an imploring "No," and then said, "OK, OK. Forgive me."

"Now that you're using your head," he responded. "I've

got a proposal to make to you."

Curious about what he was going to tell me, I egged him on childishly. He said he would do it with me only if nothing came of it, if there'd be nothing between us but sex, which we'd seek out only when we had the desire for it. I believed that in the long run even a porno novel might metamorphose into a tale of love and affection, which, absent at the start, could develop with practice. And so I prostrated myself before his will insofar as it complied with my whims: I shall be his little sex toy with an expiry date; when he gets fed up, he'll just get rid of me. Seeing that my first time would involve a true and proper agreement (though without a document that confirms and bears witness to it) between one party who is much too cunning and another who is much too curious and eager, I accepted the terms with a bowed head and a heart on the verge of exploding.

I'm hoping, however, for a positive outcome because I want to preserve the memory of it forever. I want it to be lovely, brilliant, poetic.

3:18 p.m.

My body feels destroyed and heavy, incredibly heavy. It's as though something very huge has fallen on top of me and squashed me. I'm not referring to physical pain, but to a different kind, inside. I didn't feel any physical pain even when I was on top.

This morning I took my scooter out of the garage and went to his house in the centre of town. It was early, half the town was still asleep, and the roads were nearly empty. Every so often some truck driver would blast his horn and toss me a compliment. I'd smile a little because I thought other people could perceive my happiness, which always makes me more lovely and radiant.

When I arrived at his house, I looked at my watch and realized I was tremendously early, as usual. So I sat on the scooter, opened my book bag, and took out my Greek text to go over the lesson I should've reviewed in class this very morning (if only my teacher knew I skipped school to go to bed with a boy!). I was anxious, all the same, and leafed back and forth through the book without being able to read a word. I felt my heart pounding and the blood flowing through my veins, racing beneath my skin. I laid down the book and looked at myself in the rearview mirror. I thought my pink teardrop glasses would charm him and my black poncho would knock him dead. I smiled, biting my lip, and felt proud of myself. It was just five minutes to nine; it wouldn't be a big deal if I buzzed early.

Just after I pressed the buzzer, I glimpsed his naked back in the window. He raised the blind, scowled, and said with a hard, ironic tone, "You've still got five minutes. Wait there; I'll call you at nine on the dot." At that moment I laughed stupidly, but in thinking it over now, I realize he wanted to send a very clear message about who was setting the rules and who had to follow them.

At exactly nine he came out on the balcony and said, "You can enter."

On the stairs I smelled the odour of cat piss and flowers left to wither. I heard a door open and dashed up the steps two at a time because I didn't want to be late. He'd left the door open, and I entered, softly calling his name. I heard noises in the kitchen and headed there, but he came to meet me and stopped me with a kiss on the lips, quick but pleasurable. It brought back his strawberry taste.

"Go in there," he said, pointing to the first room on the right. "I'll come in a minute."

I went into his room, which was an utter mess. He had

obviously just rolled out of bed. The walls were covered with licence plates from American cars, posters of manga cartoons, and random photos from his trips. On the bedside table stood a photo of him as a child. I touched it gently, but he put it face down, telling me I shouldn't look at it.

He grabbed me by the shoulders and spun me around, giving me the once-over. Then he complained, "What the hell are you wearing?"

"Fuck off, Daniele," I replied, wounded once again.

The phone rang, and he left the room to answer it. I didn't quite hear what he was saying, just muffled words and repressed laughter. "She's waiting for me. I'll take a peek and tell you."

At this point he put his head around the door and looked at me before he went back to the phone and said, "She's standing next to the bed with her hands in her pockets. I'm going to screw her now, and I'll tell you about it later. Ciao."

He returned with a smiling face, and I responded with a nervous smile.

Without saying a word he lowered the shutter and locked the door to his room. He looked at me for a moment and dropped his trousers, remaining in his underwear.

"Well?" he said with a scowl. "What are you doing still dressed? Are you going to take off your clothes or not?"

He laughed as I got undressed, and once I was naked, he nodded and said, "Not bad, after all. I've made a deal with a good-looking cunt." I didn't smile this time, I was nervous, I looked at my pure white arms shining in the faint sunlight that came through the window. He started kissing me on the neck and gradually moved lower, over my breasts and then the Secret, where already the River Lethe had begun to flow.

"Why don't you shave it?" he murmured.

"No," I said just as softly, "I like it better like this."

Lowering my head I noticed he was aroused, and so I

asked him if he wanted to begin.

"How would you like to do it?" he asked without hesitation.

"I don't know," I answered with a twinge of shame, "you tell me . . . I've never done it."

I lay down on the cold sheets of his unmade bed. Daniele flopped on top of me, looked me straight in the eyes, and said, "Get on top."

"Will it hurt me to be on top?" I asked in a tone that was almost reproachful.

"Who cares?" he exclaimed without looking at me.

I clambered on top of him and guided his lance to the centre of my body. I felt a slight pain, but nothing terrible. Feeling him inside me didn't provoke the frenzy I had expected. On the contrary, his sex just gave me an annoying, burning sensation, but I felt obliged to stay glued to him like that.

No groan issued from my lips, which were clenched in a smile. Letting him see my pain would have meant expressing those feelings he didn't want to acknowledge. He wanted to make use of my body, not penetrate my light.

"Come on, little one, I won't hurt you," he said.

"Don't worry, I'm not afraid. But shouldn't you be on top?" I asked with a faint smile. He sighed and agreed, throwing himself on top of me.

"Do you feel anything?" he asked as he started to move slowly.

"No," I answered, thinking he meant pain.

"How can you say no? Is it the condom?"

"I don't know," I continued, "I don't feel anything bad."

He looked at me with disgust and said, "You're no fucking virgin!"

I didn't respond immediately. I looked at him, shocked. "Sorry, but what exactly do you mean?"

"Who did you do it with?" he asked as he leaped from

the bed and picked up the clothes that were scattered across the floor.

"No one, I swear!" I raised my voice.

"We're finished for today."

There's no point telling the rest, Diary. I left without even the energy to cry or scream, with only an infinite sadness that wrenches my heart and little by little devours it.

6 March 2001

Today at lunch my mother gave me one of her inquiring looks and demanded to know why I was so preoccupied.

"It's school," I sighed. "They're loading me down with assignments."

My father kept shovelling in the spaghetti, lifting his eyes only to catch the latest drama in Italian politics on the news. I wiped my lips on the napkin, spotting it with gravy. Then I dashed out of the kitchen as my mother railed that I never showed any respect for anything or anyone, at my age she was responsible and cleaned napkins instead of dirtying them.

"Yeah, right!" I shouted from the next room. I turned down the bed and curled up beneath the covers, soaking the sheets with my tears.

The smell of softener mixed with the gross smell of the mucus that was filling my nose. I wiped it with the palm of my hand and dried my tears. My eyes lit on the portrait of me hanging on the wall: it was done not too long ago by a Brazilian painter in Taormina. As I was walking past him, he stopped me and said, "You have such a beautiful face, let me draw you. I'll do it for free."

And while his pencil sketched lines on the sheet of paper,

his eyes sparkled and smiled in place of his lips, which remained closed.

"Why do you think I have a beautiful face?" I asked him as I kept the pose.

"Because it expresses beauty, candour, innocence, spirituality," he replied, tracing broad gestures with his hands.

Beneath the covers I recalled the painter's words, as well as that morning when I lost what the old Brazilian had found so special in me. I lost it between sheets that were too cold and beneath the hands of someone who devours my very heart, which has now stopped beating. Dead. I do have a heart, Diary, even if he doesn't notice it, even if perhaps no one ever will. And before I open it, I shall give my body to any man who comes along, for two reasons: because in savouring me he might taste my rage and bitterness and therefore experience a modicum of tenderness; and because he might fall so deeply in love with my passion that he won't be able to do without it. Only then shall I give myself utterly, without hesitation, without restraint, so as not to lose the tiniest scrap of what I have always desired. I shall hold him tight within my arms and tend him like a rare and delicate flower, careful lest a gust of wind suddenly wilt him. I swear it.

9 April 2001

The days are improving. This year spring has exploded beyond measure. One day I awake and find the flowers blooming, the air warmer, as the sea gathers the sky's reflection and transforms it into an intense blue. Almost every morning I take my scooter to school. The cold is still biting, but the sun holds out the promise that later the temperature will rise. Rising up from the sea are the

Faraglioni, the rocks that the cyclops Polyphemus hurled at Odysseus (masquerading as "Nobody") after the Greek had blinded him. Nailed to the sea floor, they have stood there from time immemorial, and neither wars nor earthquakes nor even Etna's violent eruptions have ever caused them to sink. They rise impressively, erect over the water, and bring to mind how much mediocrity, how much sheer pettiness exists in the world. We talk, walk, eat, complete every action that human beings must complete, but, unlike the Faraglioni, we don't remain in the same place, unchanged. We degenerate, Diary, wars kill us, earthquakes debilitate us, lava engulfs us, and love betrays us. And we aren't even immortal. But is this not, perhaps, a good thing?

Yesterday the rocks of Polyphemus stood watching us as he moved convulsively on my body, ignoring my shivers from the cold and my averted eyes, which were pointed toward the moon's reflection in the water. We did everything in silence, as always, in the same way, every time. His face was thrust over my shoulder, and I felt his breath on my neck, no longer warm but cold. His saliva bathed every inch of my skin as if a slow, lazy snail had left his slimy track. His skin no longer recalled the golden, dewy skin I had kissed one summer morning. His lips no longer tasted of strawberry; they lacked any taste at all. At the moment when he offered me his secret potion, he voiced his usual croak of pleasure, increasingly a grunt. He detached himself from my body and stretched out on the towel beside mine, sighing as if he had freed himself from some cumbersome weight. Lying on my side, I studied the curves of his back and marvelled at them; I noted the slow approach of my hand, but immediately withdrew the gesture, fearful of his reaction. I gazed long at him and the Faraglioni, one eye on him, the other on the rocks; then shifting my gaze, I noticed the moon in the middle and stared at it, lost in wonder, squinting to bring its roundness and indescribable colour into sharper focus.

All of a sudden I turned around, as if I had unexpectedly realized something, some mystery till then beyond my grasp. "I don't love you," I murmured, almost to myself.

I didn't even have time to think it.

He slowly turned, opened his eyes, and asked, "What the fuck did you say?"

I looked at him for a moment, my face set, motionless, and in a louder voice I said, "I don't love you."

He frowned, drawing his eyebrows closer together. Then he shouted, "Who the fuck ever asked you to?"

We remained silent, and he again turned his back to me. I heard a car door close and then a couple's muted laughter. Daniele turned toward them and, annoyed, said, "What the fuck do these people want? Why don't they screw somewhere else and leave me in peace?"

"Don't they have the right to screw where they want?" I said, studying the sheen of the clear polish on my fingernails.

"Listen, babe, you don't have to tell me what other people can or can't do. I decide, only me. I've decided for you too, and I'll always decide."

While he was speaking, I turned away, annoyed, and lay down on the wet towel. He shook my shoulders angrily and emitted some indecipherable sounds through clenched teeth. I didn't move; every muscle in my body was still.

"You can't treat me like this!" he screamed. "You can't not give a damn about me. When I talk, you have to listen, you can't turn away. Understand?"

Then I suddenly turned and grabbed his wrists. They felt weak in my hands. I pitied him; my heart was aching.

"I would listen to you for hours on end," I said softly, "if only you spoke to me, if only you let me."

I saw and felt his body go slack. His eyes squeezed tight, then looked downward.

He burst into tears and covered his face with his hands,

ashamed. Once again he curled up on the towel, and once
again, with his legs folded, he resembled a defenceless,
innocent child.

I gave him a kiss on the cheek, folded my towel quietly
and carefully, gathered up all my things, and slowly headed
toward the couple. They were locked in an embrace,
nuzzling each other's necks, smelling each other's scent. I
stood watching them for a moment, and amidst the low roar
of the waves I heard a whispered "I love you".

They escorted me back home. I thanked them,
apologizing for the interruption, but they were reassuring,
insisting they were happy to help me.

Just now, Diary, as I was writing to you, I felt guilty. I left
him on the damp beach weeping bitter, pitiful tears; I
deserted him like a coward. He might even get sick. But I
did it all for him, as well as me. He has often left me in
tears, and rather than hug me he has sent me away with his
mockery. So it isn't such a tragedy for him to be left alone.
Nor is it for me.

30 April 2001

I'm happy, happy, happy! It hasn't happened the way it
should, and yet I'm happy. No one ever calls me, no one
comes looking for me, and yet I'm oozing joy from every
pore, I'm impossibly content. I've banished all my paranoias.
No more do I anxiously wait for his phone call; no more do
I suffer the anguish of having him on top of me, wriggling
all over without giving a damn about my body and me. No
more do I have to lie to my mother when, after I return
home, she asks me where I've been. Like clockwork I would
reply with just any old story: downtown to have a beer, the
cinema, the theatre. Before going to sleep I would let my

imagination run wild and think of what I would've done if I had really gone to those places. I would've amused myself, certainly, would've met people, would've had a life that wasn't just school, home, and sex with Daniele. And now I want this other life, it doesn't matter what it takes, now I want someone who is interesting to Melissa. The solitude might destroy me, but I don't find that frightening. I am my own best friend, I couldn't ever betray myself, never abandon myself. But maybe I could hurt myself, yes, just maybe I could do that. Not because I would enjoy doing it, but because I want to punish myself somehow. Yet how does a girl like me love and punish herself at the same time? It's a contradiction, Diary, I do realize. But never have love and hate been so close, so complicit, so deep inside me.

7 July 2001
12:38 am

Today I saw him again. And once again – for the last time, I hope – he abused my feelings. He started it all, as always, and finished it the same way. I'm stupid, Diary, I shouldn't ever have let him get near me again.

5 August 2001

It's finished, forever. And I'm delighted to say that I'm not finished, in fact I'm starting my life over again.

11 September 2001
3:25 pm

Maybe Daniele is watching the same images on TV, the same ones as me.

28 September 2001
9:10 am

School started a little while ago, and already the air is thick with strikes, demonstrations, and meetings over the usual issues. Already I'm imagining the reddened faces of the politicians when they clash with the protesters. The first assembly of the year will begin in a few hours, and the issue is globalization. Right now I'm sitting in a classroom during a period with a substitute teacher; behind me sit some of my schoolmates gabbing about the speaker who will lead this morning's meeting. They say he's not only very smart but good-looking, with an angelic face. When one girl says she's much less interested in the intellect than in the face, they burst into giggles. They're the same girls who went around talking trash about me a few months ago, saying I'd given it up to some guy who wasn't my boyfriend. I'd confided in one of them, told her everything about Daniele, and she'd hugged me, uttering an "I'm so sorry" that was obviously hypocritical.

"What's so funny? Wouldn't you let a guy like that bang you?" asks the girl who expressed more interest in the face.

"No, I'd rather rape him," answers another with a laugh.

"What about you, Melissa?" she asks. "What would you do?"

I turned around and told them I don't know him, and

therefore I don't feel like doing anything. Now I hear them laughing, and their laughter blends with the shrill, metallic sound of the bell that signals the end of the hour.

4:35 pm

Perched on the platform built for the assembly, I didn't care about the demolished Customs building or the torched McDonald's, even though I'd been chosen to write a report on the event. I was seated in the centre of the long table; on either side of me were the representatives of the opposing sides. The guy with the angelic face sat next to me, gnawing on a pen in the most obscene way. And while the confirmed rightist engaged with the tenacious leftist, my eyes studied the blue pen wedged between his teeth.

"Write down my name among the participants," he said at a certain point, his face bent over a slip of paper filled with notes.

"What is your name?" I asked tactfully.

"Roberto," he said, although this time he looked at me, surprised that I didn't already know it.

He stood up to speak. His speech was strong and compelling. I watched him as he moved with self-confidence, holding the microphone and the pen. The extremely attentive audience smiled at his ironic quips, which he made at just the right moments. He's a law student, I thought, which explains his rhetorical skills. Every so often he would turn to look at me. Somewhat mischievously, although in the most unaffected manner, I started unbuttoning my blouse from the neck down, revealing the white swell of my breasts. Perhaps he noticed my gesture. At any rate, he began to turn more frequently, and with a mixture of curiosity and slight embarrassment he started making eyes at me, or at least so I thought. After finishing his speech, he sat down again and stuck the pen back in his mouth, ignoring the applause that was directed at him. Then he turned toward me – I had meanwhile gone back to writing my report – and said, "I don't recall your name."

I felt like playing. "I still haven't told you," I replied.

He lifted his head a bit and said, "Right . . ."

I smiled and watched him resume taking notes, pleased that he might be waiting for me to tell him my name.

"Aren't you going to tell me?" he asked, scrutinizing my face.

I beamed. "Melissa," I said.

"Mmmm . . . Your name is the Greek for 'bee'. Do you like honey?"

"Too sweet," I replied. "I prefer stronger tastes."

He shook his head, smiled, and each of us continued writing on our own. After a while he stood up to smoke a cigarette, and I saw him laugh and gesture excitedly to another guy (who was also quite handsome). At times he would glance at me and smile, letting the cigarette dangle from his mouth. From a distance he appeared thinner, and his hair seemed soft and scented, bronze-coloured ringlets that fell gently on his face. He stood leaning against the streetlight, shifting all his weight to one hip, which he seemed to be holding up with the hand in his trouser pocket. A green-checked shirt flounced out, disarranged, and round glasses completed his intellectual look. I'd seen his friend a few times outside of school, handing out leaflets. He invariably had a small cigar in his mouth, lit or not.

When the meeting ended, I was gathering the sheets of paper scattered on the table – I had to submit them with my report – and Roberto returned. He squeezed my hand and said goodbye with a broad smile.

"*Arrivederci*, comrade!"

I started laughing and confessed that I liked being called comrade, it's amusing.

"Come, come!" said the assistant principal, clapping his hands. "What are you doing there chattering away? Do you not see that the assembly has ended?"

Today I'm happy. I had this lovely encounter and hope it doesn't end here. You know, Diary, I truly persevere if I want to achieve something. Now I want his phone number, and I'm sure I'll manage to get it. After his number I'll want what you already know – namely, to inhabit his thoughts. But before that happens you know what I must do.

10 October 2001
5:15 pm

It's a wet, melancholy day. The sky is grey, the sun a faded smear. This morning there was some light rain, but now a few flashes of lightning would be enough to unleash a downpour. Still, the weather doesn't make a difference to me: I'm very happy.

Stationed at the school entrance were the usual vultures wanting to sell you books or to persuade you with leaflets, undeterred even by the rain. Roberto's friend was there, a cigar in his mouth, wearing a green raincoat and handing out red flyers, a smile stamped on his face. When he approached to give me one as well, I stared at him, flabbergasted, since I didn't know what to do, how to act. I mumbled a timid thanks and dragged my heels, thinking that a golden opportunity like this wouldn't happen again. I wrote my number on the flyer, turned around, and handed it back to him.

"Why are you returning it? Why don't you just throw

it away like everybody else?" he asked me, smiling.

"No, I want you to give it to Roberto," I said.

Bewildered, he protested, "But Roberto has hundreds of these."

I bit my lip. "Roberto will be interested in what's written on the back."

"Ah, I understand." He seemed even more bewildered. "Don't worry, I'll see him later, and he'll get it."

"*Grazie!*" I'd have preferred to give him a loud kiss on the cheek.

As I was leaving, I heard someone call me. I turned, and it was him, breaking into a run.

"I forgot," he panted, "my name's Pino, pleased to meet you. You're Melissa, right?"

"Yes, Melissa. I see you couldn't wait to read the back of the flyer."

"Well . . . What of it?" he said, smiling. "Curiosity is a sign of intelligence. Are you curious?"

I closed my eyes and said, "Immensely."

"You see, then you're intelligent."

My ego appeased, sated with happiness, I said goodbye and headed toward the piazza in front of the school, a hangout that was now half-empty because of the nasty weather. I didn't start the scooter right away. The traffic at that hour is terrible, even on a motorino. A few minutes later my phone rang.

"Yes?"

"Ummm . . . Ciao, it's Roberto."

"Whoa! . . . Ciao."

"You surprised me, you know?"

"I like to take chances. You could have not called me. I ran the risk of getting a door slammed in my face."

"You did the right thing. I would've come to ask after you one of these days. Except that . . . you know . . . my girlfriend goes to the same school."

"So you're taken."

"Yes, but that doesn't matter."

"It doesn't matter to me either."

"Tell me, what made you look for me?"

"What would make you come looking for me?"

"I asked you first."

"I want to get to know you better, spend some time with you."

Silence.

"Now it's your turn."

"Same here. As long as you know the premise: I'm already committed."

"I don't really believe in commitments. They end when you stop believing in them."

"Feel like meeting up tomorrow morning?"

"No, not tomorrow, I have school. Let's meet Friday – the day of the strike. Where?"

"In front of the university cafeteria at 10:30."

"I'll be there."

"Ciao, then, till Friday."

"Till Friday. *Un bacio.*"

14 October 2001
5:30 pm

As usual I arrived incredibly early. The weather has been the same for four days, an incredible monotony.

From the cafeteria came the smell of garlic, and from where I stood I could hear the cooks making a racket with the pots and bad-mouthing some co-workers. A few students passed by and winked at me; I pretended not to see them. I was more attentive to the cooks' conversation than my thoughts. I was calm, not in the least nervous; I let myself be swept away by the external world, and I didn't pay much attention to me.

He arrived in his yellow car, wrapped up in the most exaggerated way, with an enormous scarf covering half his face, leaving only his glasses uncovered.

"So I won't be recognized, you know how it is . . . my girlfriend. We'll use the back roads," he said once I'd got into the car. "It'll take a bit longer, but at least there won't be any risk."

The rain beat harder on the windscreen; I thought it might shatter. We were headed for his summer home on the slopes of Etna, outside the city. The brown, withered branches of the trees tore tiny cracks in the cloudy sky; flocks of birds flew laboriously through the dense rainfall, yearning to reach some warmer place. I too wanted to soar in order to reach a warmer spot. Yet I felt no yearning: it seemed as if I were leaving home to start a new job that was far from exciting – a dutiful, laborious job.

"Open the glove compartment. There should be some CDs."

I found a couple and chose Carlos Santana.

We talked about my school and his university, then about us.

"I don't want you to think badly of me," I said.

"Are you joking? That would be like thinking badly of myself. We're both doing the same thing, in the same way. For me it might be even more dishonourable, since I'm spoken for. But you see, she – "

"Doesn't give you any," I interrupted with a smile.

"Exactly," he said with the same smile.

He entered a narrow, badly paved road and stopped before a huge green gate. He climbed out of the car and opened the gate. When he got back inside, I noticed the face of Che Guevara printed on his drenched T-shirt.

"Fuck!" he complained. "It's still autumn, but the weather

is already so lousy." Then he turned to me and asked, "Aren't you a little excited?"

I closed my lips so tightly that I wrinkled my chin. I shook my head and after a brief pause said, "No, not at all."

To reach the door I covered my head with my bag. Running in the rain, we laughed non-stop, like two idiots.

The house was completely dark. When I entered, I felt an icy cold. I groped my way in the pitch darkness; he was evidently used to it. He was familiar with every corner and therefore walked with a certain confidence. I planted myself in a spot where there seemed to be more light and made out a couch, where I placed my bag.

Roberto came up from behind, turned me around, and kissed me, thrusting his entire tongue into my mouth. I found this kiss a bit repulsive; it wasn't at all like Daniele's. He was swapping spit with me, letting it trickle from our lips. I backed off tactfully, without revealing my disgust, and wiped my mouth with the palm of my hand. He took me by the same hand and led me into the bedroom, which was just as dark and just as cold.

"Can't you switch on the light?" I asked while he was kissing my neck.

"No, I like it better like this."

He left me on the huge bed, knelt down, and removed his shoes. I was neither excited nor impassive. I felt I was doing everything just to please him.

He undressed me as if I were a mannequin in a window display, the way a fast, detached shop assistant strips the dummy and leaves it bare.

He was shocked to see my stockings. "You're wearing thigh-highs?" he asked.

"Yes, always," I replied.

"You filthy pig!" he roared.

I was embarrassed by his comment, so out of place, but I was even more struck by his transformation from a polite, well-bred young man to a coarse, vulgar beast. His eyes were flaming, ravenous, his hands rummaged around beneath my blouse, inside my panties.

"Do you want me to keep them on?" I asked to comply with his wishes.

"Definitely, leave them, you're dirtier like this."

My cheeks flushed again, but now I felt my fireplace start to blaze, and reality gradually receded. Passion was getting the upper hand.

I got down from the bed, and my feet touched the smooth, incredibly cold floor. I waited for him to take me and do what he wanted.

"Suck my dick, slut," he whispered.

I ignored my shame, immediately banished it, and did what he asked me to do. I felt his member turn hard and swollen. He grabbed me by the armpits and lifted me to the bed.

He positioned me on top of him like a defenceless doll and aimed his long lance toward my sex, still so little opened, so little wet.

"I want to make you feel pain. Come on, scream, let me hear how I'm hurting you."

There was in fact pain, I felt the walls burning, and the dilation occurred against my will.

I screamed as the dark room spun around me. My embarrassment had vanished and in its place was only the desire to make him mine.

"If I scream," I thought, "he'll be happy, he asked me to do it. I'll do anything he tells me."

I screamed and felt pain, no trace of pleasure passed through me. He, however, exploded, his voice was transformed, and his words turned obscene and vulgar.

He hurled them at me, and they pierced me with a violence that exceeded even his penetration.

Then everything returned to the way it was before. He

picked up his glasses from the bedside table, took off the condom with a tissue and threw it away, calmly dressed, caressed my head, and when we got into the car, we talked about bin Laden and Bush as if nothing had happened.

25 October 2001

Roberto calls me often. He says hearing me fills him with joy and the desire to make love. He says the latter in a low voice, partly because he doesn't want to be heard, partly because he's embarrassed to admit it. I tell him that I feel the same way, that I often think about him when I touch myself. It isn't true, Diary. I say it only to stroke his ego; he's full of himself. He's forever saying, "I know I'm a good lover. Women really like me."

He's an arrogant angel, he's irresistible. His image hounds me during the day, but I think of him more as the polite young man than as the passionate lover. And when he is transformed, he makes me smile: I think he knows quite well how to maintain his equilibrium, how to be different people at different times. Unlike me, always the same, always identical. My passion is everywhere, so is my cunning.

1 December 2001

I told him my birthday is the day after tomorrow, and he exclaimed, "Great. Then we'll have to celebrate in an appropriate fashion."

I smiled and said, "Robi, we just celebrated yesterday. Aren't you satisfied?"

"Uh, no. I meant your birthday should be special. You know Pino, don't you?"

"Yes, of course," I replied.

"Do you like him?"

Worried about saying something that would distance him from me, I hesitated a little, then decided to tell the truth: "Yes, quite a lot."

"Perfect. I'll come to pick you up the day after tomorrow."

"OK." I shut my phone, curious about this strange excitement of his. I trust him.

3 December 2001
4:30 am

My sixteenth birthday. I want to stop right here and not go any further. At sixteen I'm mistress of my actions, but also the victim of chance and unpredictability.

When I left the house, I noticed Roberto wasn't alone in his yellow car. I saw the black cigar, indistinct in the darkness, and understood everything.

"You could at least stay home on your birthday," my mother said before I went out, but I didn't listen to her. I softly closed the door and left without answering.

The arrogant angel looked at me with a smile, and I climbed into the car, pretending I hadn't noticed Pino in the back seat.

"Well?" Roberto asked. "Don't you have anything to say?" He nodded toward the back.

I turned and saw Pino, wasted, his eyes red, his pupils dilated. I smiled at him and asked, "Did you smoke?"

He nodded yes, and Roberto added, "He also drank an entire bottle of grappa."

"Splendid," I said. "He's in great shape."

The lights of the city were reflected on the car windows.

The shops were still open; the owners eagerly awaited Christmas. Couples and families strolled on the pavements, unaware that I was riding in the car with two men who were taking me to some strange place.

We crossed Via Etnea, and I saw the Duomo, the cathedral illuminated by white lights and surrounded by impressive palm trees. The river flows beneath this street, hidden by volcanic rock. It is silent, imperceptible. Just like my silent, docile thoughts, skilfully concealed behind my armour. They flow, eating away at me.

In the morning the fish market is held nearby. You can smell the scent of the sea on the fishermen's hands, their nails blackened by entrails. They fill a bucket with water and splash it on the cold, gleaming bodies of animals that are still living, still quivering. We were heading precisely in that direction, even though at night the atmosphere changes. When I climbed out of the car, I realized the scent of the sea metamorphoses into the scent of hashish, kids pierced with studs and rings replace the old, tanned fishermen, and life continues to be life, always, no matter what.

An ancient woman with a horrible odour passed by me, dressed in red and holding a cat that was red too, bony and blind in one eye. She was chanting a singsong verse in Sicilian, which went something like this:

> *Via Etnea is the place to stroll:*
> *A wealth of light, if truth be told.*
> *Hordes of people milling about;*
> *Those guys in jeans just hanging out.*
> *They strut their stuff as on display*
> *In front of each and every café.*
> *At night Catania so lovely seems,*
> *Shining beneath the bright moonbeams.*
> *The mountain top is red with fire;*
> *Its heat to lovers proves most dire.*

She walked like a ghost, at a snail's pace, her eyes staring wildly, and I stood watching her, my curiosity piqued, as I waited for them to get out of the car. The woman brushed against the sleeve of my overcoat, and I felt a weird shudder. Our eyes met for the briefest instant, but it was so intense and so eloquent that I was afraid, really afraid, crazed. Her lively, sidelong glance wasn't in the least obtuse. It spoke: "Inside you shall discover death. You shall never recover your heart, girl, you shall die, and some man will toss earth on your grave. Not even a flower, not a single one."

I had gooseflesh; that witch had cast a spell on me. But I didn't heed her. I smiled at the two guys who came toward me, handsome and dangerous.

Pino could barely stand up. He remained silent the entire time. Nor did Roberto and I speak as much as we usually did.

Roberto pulled a huge ring of keys from his trouser pocket and slipped one into the lock. The portal creaked; he had to apply some force to open it, and finally it closed noisily behind us.

I didn't say a word; I didn't have any questions. I knew quite well what we were about to do. We climbed a timeworn staircase. The walls of the palazzo seemed so fragile I was afraid they might suddenly give way and kill us; the countless cracks let in a white light, making the blue walls appear diaphanous. We stopped at a door through which I could hear music.

"Is someone here?" I asked.

"No," Roberto replied, "we forgot to switch off the radio before we left."

Pino immediately went to the bathroom, leaving the door open. I watched him piss, holding his limp, wrinkled member. Roberto went into the other room to lower the volume, and I stayed in the corridor, curiously examining all the rooms I could spy from there.

The arrogant angel returned, smiling. He kissed me on the mouth, and pointing toward a room, he said, "Await us in the cell of desires. We shall arrive soon."

"The cell of desires," I giggled. "What a strange name to call a room where you screw!"

I entered the narrow room. Tacked to the walls were hundreds of photos of nude models, pages from porno magazines, x-rated Japanese cartoons, and positions from the *Kama Sutra*. Predictably, a red flag with Che's face was unfurled on the ceiling.

"Where have I ended up?" I thought. "Some sort of sex museum. Who in the world owns this house?"

Roberto arrived with some black cloth in his hand. He turned me around and blindfolded me with the cloth. As he turned me back to face him, he exclaimed with a laugh, "You look like the goddess Fortune."

I heard the click of the light switch and could no longer see anything.

I discerned steps and whispers. Then two hands pulled down my jeans and removed my turtleneck sweater and my bra. I remained in a G-string, thigh-highs, and stiletto-heeled boots. I saw myself blindfolded and naked, saw on my face only my red lips, which would soon get a taste of them.

Suddenly the hands multiplied, becoming four. It was easy to distinguish them, since two were above, fondling my breasts, and two were below, rubbing my sex through the string and caressing my bottom. I couldn't get a whiff of Pino's alcohol; perhaps he had brushed his teeth in the bathroom. While I imagined myself at the mercy of their hands and began to get excited, I felt the touch of an ice-cold object from behind, a glass. The hands continued to feel me up, but the glass pressed harder against my skin. Frightened, I asked, "Who the hell is that?"

Muffled laughter in the background, then an unfamiliar voice: "Your barman, precious. Don't worry: I've only brought you a drink."

He drew the glass to my mouth, and I slowly sipped some cream liqueur. I licked my lips, and another mouth kissed me passionately while the hands continued to caress me, and the barman gave me another sip. A fourth man was kissing me.

"What a beautiful ass you have," said an unfamiliar voice, "soft, spotless, firm. May I give you a bite?"

I smiled at the comical request and replied, "Just do it, don't ask. But there's one thing I want to know: how many are you?"

"Relax, *amore*," said another voice at my shoulder. And I felt a tongue lick the vertebrae in my back. The image I now had of myself was more seductive: blindfolded, half naked, five men licking me, caressing me, lusting brazenly for my body. I was the centre of attention, and they did with me what one is permitted to do in the cell of desires. I didn't hear a word, only sighs and caresses.

When a finger slowly slipped inside my Secret, I felt a sudden warmth and realized that reason was abandoning me. I surrendered to the touch of their hands, yet I was keen to know who and what they were. What if the pleasure I experienced were the work of a slobbering, hideously ugly man? At that moment it meant nothing to me. Now I feel ashamed, Diary, but I know regretting things after you've done them is pointless.

"Perfect," Roberto said finally. "Only the last component is missing."

"What?" I asked.

"Don't worry. You can remove the blindfold. We'll play another game now."

I hesitated a moment to remove the blindfold, but then I slowly slipped it off my head and saw that Roberto and I were alone in the room.

"Where have they gone?" I asked, surprised.

"They're waiting for us in the other room."

"What is that one called?" I asked, amused.

"Mmmm . . . the smoking room. We'll roll a joint."

I desperately wanted with all my might to take off and leave them there. The pause in the action had dampened my excitement, and reality appeared in all its crudeness. But I couldn't leave: I had already started and had to finish at any cost. I had to do it for them.

I glimpsed the silhouettes etched in the darkness, illuminated only by three candles placed on the floor. From what little I could make out, the guys present in the room didn't appear ugly, and this consoled me.

There was a round table surrounded by chairs. The arrogant angel was seated.

"Do you smoke?" Pino asked me.

"No, thanks, I never smoke."

"But tonight you will," said the barman. I could perceive that he was well-built, slender and shapely. His skin was dark, and his curly hair shoulder-length.

"No, I'm sorry to disappoint you. When I say no, it's no. I've never smoked, I won't smoke now, and I don't know if I'll smoke in future. I find it unnecessary, so I'll leave it to you."

"But at least you won't deprive us of a beautiful sight," said Roberto, clapping his hand on the wooden table. "Sit here."

I sat at the table with my legs spread, the heels of my boots nailed to the floor and my sex visible to all. Roberto approached the chair and pointed the lit candle toward my pubic area to illuminate it.

As he rolled the joint, he glanced back and forth from the fragrant grass to my Secret. His eyes were glistening.

"Touch yourself," he commanded me. I slowly slipped a finger in my wound, and he stopped working on the joint, yielding to the sight of my sex.

Someone approached from behind. He kissed my

shoulders, took me in his arms, and jammed me against his body, trying to enter me with his lance. I was disarmed. My eyes downcast and lifeless. I didn't want to look.

"Hey hey, no," said Pino. "We talked about this before. Nobody penetrates her tonight."

The barman went into the next room to find the black cloth that had covered my eyes. They blindfolded me again, and a hand forced me to kneel down.

"Now, Melissa, we shall pass the joint." I heard Roberto's voice. "Whoever is holding it will snap his fingers and touch your head, so you will know that it has arrived. You must draw near, when we tell you, and take it in your mouth until it comes. Five times, Melissa, five. Henceforth we shall no longer speak. Perform your task well."

Five different tastes clashed on my palate, the five flavours of five men. Every flavour told its story, every potion bespoke my shame. During those moments I had the illusory sensation that pleasure was not only physical, that it might be beauty, joy, freedom. And kneeling naked in their midst I sensed that I belonged to another, unknown world. But then, after I exited that room, my heart was in shreds, and I experienced an unspeakable shame.

They then abandoned me on the bed, and my body felt numb. On the desk in the narrow room my phone started flashing, and I knew the call was coming from home. It was already two-thirty in the morning. But then someone entered, stretched out on top of me, and screwed me. Another followed him and pointed his penis toward my mouth. As soon as one had finished, another would unload his whitish liquid on me. One after another. Sighs, moans, grunts. And quiet tears.

I returned home full of sperm, my makeup smeared. My mother was waiting for me, asleep on the couch.

She was too sleepy to upbraid me about the hour, so she just nodded and headed toward her bedroom.

I entered the bathroom, looked at myself in the mirror, and no longer saw the image of that girl who took such delight in examining herself a few years ago. I saw sad eyes, rendered even more pitiful by the black liner that streamed down my cheeks. I saw a mouth that had been violated so many times tonight and had lost its freshness. I felt invaded, fouled by foreign bodies.

Then I brushed my hair a hundred times, as princesses do, my mother always says, with my vagina even now, as I write in the dead of night, still smelling of sex.

4 December 2001
12:45 pm

"Did you have fun last night?" my mother asked me this morning, drowning out the gurgle of the coffee pot with a yawn.

I shrugged and responded that I'd spent the night just like so many others.

"Your clothes had a strange smell," she said with her usual look of wanting to know everything, especially where it concerns me.

Frightened, I abruptly turned my back on her and bit my lip. I thought she might have picked up the scent of sperm.

"What kind of smell?" I asked, feigning composure, mindlessly observing the sun through the kitchen window.

"Smoke. It smelled like marijuana," she said with an expression of disgust.

Relieved, I turned around, smiled slightly, and said, "Well, people were smoking in the club last night. I couldn't possibly ask them to put it out."

She gave me a surly look and said, "If you come home stoned, you won't even be allowed to go to school."

"That's fine with me," I joked. "I'll see if I can find a reliable dealer. Thanks, you've given me a great excuse to cut those shitty classes."

As if the only thing that might be harmful is hashish. I'd smoke gram after gram if it could help me shake off this strange sensation of emptiness, of nothingness. It's as if I were suspended in the air, looking down in shock at what I did yesterday. No, that wasn't me. That was the girl who doesn't love herself, who allowed herself to be touched by greedy, unfamiliar hands, who became a receptacle for the sperm of five different guys, who so defiled her soul that she can't feel pain.

I am the one who does love herself, who last night made her hair shine again with a hundred careful strokes of the brush, who rediscovered the childlike softness of her lips, and who kissed herself, sharing the love that yesterday had been denied her.

20 December 2001

A time of gifts and false smiles, of coins tossed – with a fleeting burst of good conscience – into the hands of gypsies holding babies on street corners. I don't like to buy gifts for other people; I always buy them for myself alone, perhaps because I have nobody to whom to give them. This afternoon I went out with Ernesto, a guy I met in a chat room. He immediately seemed like a kindred spirit. We exchanged phone numbers and began seeing each other like dear friends, even if he is slightly distant, absorbed by the university and his mysterious friendships.

We often go shopping together, and I'm not embarrassed when I enter a lingerie shop with him. On the contrary, he frequently buys something too.

"For my new girl," he always says. But he has never introduced me to any of them.

He seems to be on very good terms with the salesgirls. Their talk avoids the social niceties and they giggle away. I rummage through the racks, searching for things I might wear for the person who managed to fall in love with me. I keep them carefully folded in the first drawer of the dresser, intact.

In the second drawer I keep the lingerie I wear during my encounters with Roberto and his friends. Thigh-highs shredded by their fingernails, lace panties slightly frayed from being stripped off too many times by lustful hands. They attach no importance to these things; to them what matters is that I'm a slut.

In the beginning I would buy only lingerie in white lace, carefully coordinating each piece.

"Black would suit you better," Ernesto once told me. "It goes better with your colouring, the shade of your face, your skin."

I followed his advice, and from then on I bought only black lace.

I watch him take a fancy to the coloured thongs, worthy of a Brazilian dancer: shocking pink, green, electric blue. When he shops in earnest, he chooses red.

"Your girlfriends must be really weird," I tell him.

With a giggle he says, "Not as weird as you," and my ego is boosted again.

The bras are almost all padded. He never coordinates them with the panties, preferring to juxtapose colours that seem unlikely together.

Then the stockings: mine are almost always thigh-highs, crowned with a band of lace, strictly black, so they form a sharp contrast with the wintry pallor of my skin. He buys fishnets, which don't match my taste.

When Ernesto is particularly fond of a girl, he dives into the throng at a department store and buys her glittering dresses adorned with multicoloured sequins, cut with dizzying necklines and daring slits.

"How much does this girl make an hour?" I joke.

He turns serious and, without responding, goes to pay. Then I feel guilty and stop acting like stupid idiot.

Today, as we strolled through the shops, past the acid young salesgirls, the rain caught us by surprise, soaking the packages we were toting.

"Let's go under the portico!" he shouted as he seized my hand.

"Ernesto!" I said, midway between irritation and amusement. "There are no porticos on Via Etnea!"

He looked at me, bug-eyed, shrugged, and exclaimed, "Then let's go to my place!" I didn't want to go there: I learned that one of his roommates is Maurizio, a friend of Roberto's. I didn't feel like seeing him; much less did I want Ernesto to discover my secret activities.

From the place where we stood his apartment was only a few hundred yards away. We covered them at a fast clip, hand in hand. It felt great to break into a mad dash with someone who doesn't make me feel like I have to get into bed with him and let myself go, no holds barred. For once I'd like to be the one who decides: when and where to do it, how long, with how much desire.

"Is anyone home?" I whispered as I climbed the stairs with a booming echo.

"No," he replied, breathless. "They've all left for the holidays. Only Gianmaria stayed home, but he's out right now." Content, I followed him, hastily sprucing myself up in the mirror on the wall.

His place was half-empty, but the presence of four men was visible: there was a nasty smell (yes, that oppressive smell of sperm), and the rooms looked like they had been hit by a cyclone.

We flung the packages to the floor and removed our

dripping overcoats.

"Do you want one of my T-shirts? It'll take a while for your clothes to dry."

"OK," I said, "*grazie.*"

When we reached his bedroom–cum–library, he approached the wardrobe with a peculiar anxiety; and before he would open it completely, he asked me to fetch the packages from the other room.

When I returned, he quickly shut the wardrobe. Amused and soaked, I blurted, "What do you have in there? Your dead women?"

He smiled and answered, "More or less."

His answer made me curious. But he avoided other questions by tearing the packages from my hands and saying, "Come on, let me see! What did you buy, little one?"

He opened my wet box with both hands and stuck his head inside, like a child opening a Christmas gift. His eyes sparkled, and with his fingertips he drew out a pair of black panties.

"Ooh-la-la! And what do you do with these, eh? Do you wear them for someone in particular? I doubt they're part of your school uniform."

"We all have our secrets," I said ironically, aware that I was arousing his suspicions.

He marvelled at me, leaned his head slightly to the left, and softly said, "What do you mean? Let's hear: what's your secret?"

I was weary of keeping it inside me, Diary. So I told him. The expression on his face didn't change; he wore the same look of enchantment as before.

"Don't you have anything to say?" I asked, irritated.

"You've made your choices, little one. I can only tell you to go slow."

"It's too late," I said, feigning resignation. Trying to stifle my embarrassment, I burst out laughing and then said in a cheery voice, "OK, honeybunch, now it's your turn. Your secret?"

He blanched, and his eyes darted around the room, uncertain. He stood up from the faded floral sofa bed and took a few giant steps toward the wardrobe. Then he dramatically threw open one door, pointed at the clothes hanging there, and said, "These are mine."

I recognized the things; we had bought them together. The price tags had been removed, and they had clearly been worn. They were wrinkled.

"What do you mean, Ernesto?" I said quietly.

His movements slowed, his muscles relaxed, his eyes turned toward the floor.

"I buy these clothes for myself. I wear them and... I work in them."

This time I was left speechless; I really couldn't think of anything to say. Then a moment later my head was crowded with questions: You work in them? What kind of work do you do? Where do you work? Why?

He began before I could ask them. "I like to dress up as a woman. I started doing it a few years ago. I lock myself in my room, plant a video camera on the table, and dress up. I like it; it feels good. Later I watch myself on the screen and... well, I get excited. Sometimes I'll let someone else see me on film, if they ask." He was suddenly swallowed by a deep blush.

Dead silence. The only sound was the noise of the rain streaming down from the sky, forming thin wires that encaged us.

"Are you a prostitute?" I asked, not mincing words.

He nodded, immediately covering his face with both hands.

"Meli, believe me, I only do oral sex, nothing else. Someone might ask me to ... take it up the ass, but I swear, I never do it. It's to pay for my studies, you know, my parents can't afford it." He would've continued, fishing for more excuses. Anyway, I know he likes it.

"I don't blame you, Ernesto," I said after a lull. I was carefully examining the window where the droplets sparkled nervously.

"Look, everybody chooses their own life. You said it yourself a few minutes ago. Sometimes even the wrong roads can turn out to be the right ones, or vice versa. The important thing is to follow your dream, to be true to yourself, because only if we succeed in doing this can we say that we've made the best choice for ourselves. At this point, what I really want to know is why you do it." I was being a hypocrite.

Then he looked at me with tender, questioning eyes and asked, "Why do *you* do it?"

I didn't answer, but my silence spoke volumes. My conscience was screaming so loudly that to repress it I said spontaneously, without any shame, "Why don't you dress up for me?"

"Why are you asking me this?"

I myself didn't know. Slightly embarrassed, I spoke in a hushed tone: "Because it's beautiful to see two identities in the same body: man and woman in the same skin. Here's another secret: it excites me. A lot. But forgive me... it's something we both like; nobody is forcing us to do it. A pleasure can never be a mistake, right?"

I noticed from his trousers that he was aroused. He tried to hide it.

"I'll do it," he said curtly. From the wardrobe he took a dress and then a T-shirt, which he tossed to me.

"Sorry, I'd forgotten to get it for you. You can wear that."

"I'll have to undress," I said.

"Are you ashamed?"

"No, no, of course not," I replied.

As I undressed, my nudity increased his excitement. I

slipped into the huge pink T-shirt. On the front it featured a winking Marilyn with the caption "Bye Bye Baby". Together we watched my friend don his vestments, as if it were an ecstatic, sublime ceremony. He dressed with his back turned, so I could scarcely make out his movements, not to mention the G-string that parted his square buttocks. He turned to face me: black miniskirt, fishnet stockings, thigh-high boots, gold lamé top, padded bra. This is how he presented himself to me, a friend I'd always seen in Lacoste and Levi's! My excitement wasn't visible, but it was there.

His dick popped out of the flimsy G-string with no problem. He shifted it and started rubbing.

As in some performance, I stretched out on the sofa bed and eyed him attentively. I longed to touch myself, even to possess that body. Much to my amazement, I watched him masturbate as if I had assumed a male gaze. His face was rapturous, beaded with little drops of sweat. My pleasure arrived without penetration, without caresses, simply through my mind, through me.

His, however, came strong and steady, I saw him spurt and heard his gasp, which broke off when he opened his eyes.

He lay down on the sofa with me. We hugged each other and fell asleep as Marilyn rubbed her eye against Ernesto's gold lamé top.

3 January 2002
2:30 am

Another visit to the museum-like house with the same
people. This time we played a game: I was the earth, and
they were worms burrowing into it. Five different worms
dug furrows in my body, and the soil, upon my return
home, was loose and crumbly. An old yellowed nightgown,
my grandmother's, was hanging in my wardrobe. I slipped
into it and smelled the scent of softener and a time long
gone as they blended with the absurd present. I undid my
hair and let it fall to my shoulders, protected by the
comforting past. I undid it, nuzzled it, and went to bed
with a smile that quickly turned into weeping. Gentle,
tame, and meek.

9 January 2002

At Ernesto's house there aren't many secrets. I confided to
him that my experiences had provoked a desire to see one
man inside another. I really want to see two men screw. To
see them screw each other just as they've screwed me, with
the same violence, the same brutality.

I can't stop myself, I'm moving as fast as a stick swept along by the current in a river. I'm learning to say no to other people and yes to myself, learning to release the deepest part of me and let it slam against the surrounding world. I'm learning.

"Melissa, you're a continual revelation," he said, his voice still hoarse from sleep. "How can I put it? You're a mine of fantasies and imagination."

"I swear, Ernesto," I said, still hugging him, "I'd even pay." After a brief silence, I turned impatient and asked, "So?"

"So what?"

"You're from that camp. Don't you know anyone who might like to be watched?"

"Come on! What are you up to? Can't you be a nice girl and act normal?"

"Nice isn't really me," I said. "And what do you mean by acting normal?"

"Acting like a sixteen-year-old, Meli. Boy meets girl, they fall in love and have sex, everything balances out, and they live happily ever after."

"Please, in my view, that's the height of perversion!" I shouted hysterically. "Utterly dull: Saturday night in Piazza Teatro Massimo, Sunday morning breakfast at the seashore, sex strictly reserved for weekends, confiding secrets to your parents, and so on. It'd be better to stay single."

Another silence.

"I'm just not like that; I don't want to change for anybody. And you – you're one to talk!" In jest, I screamed this last bit in his face.

He laughed and caressed my head.

"Little one, I love you. I wouldn't ever want something unpleasant to happen to you."

"It'll happen to me if I don't do what I want. And I love you too."

He told me about two guys, law students in their final

year. I'll meet them tomorrow: after school, they'll come to
pick me up at Villa Bellini, in front of the fountain where
the swans swim. I'll call my mother and tell her I'll be out
all afternoon, attending a drama class.

10 January 2002
3:45 pm

"You women are idiots! Watch two men screw . . . mah!"
said Germano. He was driving. His eyes were huge and
black; his massive, finely sculpted face was crowned by the
most beautiful black ringlets, which, if not for his fair
complexion, would have made him a young African, potent
and proud. He was ensconced in the driver's seat like the
King of the Forest, tall and majestic, his long, tapering
fingers on the steering wheel. A steel ring with tribal
markings stood out against the whiteness of his skin and its
extraordinary softness.

His partner, a thin-lipped guy who sat behind me,
responded in a faint, polite voice: "Leave her alone. Can't
you see she's young? And she's so tiny. . . Look at her lovely
little face, so sweet. Are you sure you want to do this, little
one?"

I nodded.

From what I gathered, these two had agreed to the
encounter because they owed Ernesto a favour, though I didn't
have the faintest idea what exactly they were paying back. The
fact is that Germano was put out by the situation, and if he'd
had his way, he'd have left me by the side of the deserted road.
And yet an obscure enthusiasm shone in his eyes; it was a subtle
feeling that I sensed coming and going at intervals. During the
journey, silence kept us company. We were driving down a

country road, heading for Gianmaria's villa, the only place where no one would disturb us. It was an old farmhouse, built of stone and surrounded by olive and fir trees; in the distance you could see rows of vines, dead in this season. The wind gusted, and when Gianmaria got out to open the enormous iron gate, a mass of leaves dropped into the car, falling on my hair. The cold was piercing, the smell that of wet soil and leaves long left to rot in water. I clutched my handbag and stood up straight in my high-heeled boots, hugging myself against the icy chill. The tip of my nose felt frozen; my cheeks were tight, anaesthetized. We arrived at the main door, wherein the names of various children had been carved during their summer games, a sign of one's passage through time. Germano's and Gianmaria's had also been etched in the wood... I've got to run, Diary, my mother has just thrown open my door and told me I have to accompany her to visit my aunt (she broke a hip and is in the hospital).

11 January 2002

A dream I had tonight:

I'm getting off an airplane. The sky over Milano shows me a sullen, hostile face. The clinging, icy wind musses and flattens my hair, just done at the salon. In the grayish light, my face looks washed out, and my eyes seem empty, ringed by narrow phosphorescent circles that make me even weirder.

My hands are cold and white, corpselike. I arrive inside the airport and spot my reflection in a window: I take note of my face, thin and colourless, my long hair, dishevelled and at this point horrendous, my lips, clenched, hermetically sealed. I am aware of a strange, unmotivated excitement.

Then I flash on myself again, just as the reflection shows

me, but somewhere else. Instead of being in an airport, dressed in my usual designer clothes, I am suddenly in a dark, putrid cell touched by so little light I can't see what clothes I'm wearing or what kind of condition I'm in. I weep; I am alone. Outside it must be night. At the end of the corridor I glimpse a flickering light, which is nonetheless intense. No noise. The light approaches. It grows closer and closer, frightening me, since I hear no step at all. The man who arrives moves with great caution. He is tall, potent.

He rests both of his hands on the bars; I stand, drying my eyes, and go to meet him. The light of the torch illumines his face, suffusing it with a diabolical air, while his body remains in shadow. I see his enormous, ravenous eyes of some indefinable colour, and his broad lips, which are parted, permitting a glimpse of a row of pearly teeth. He lifts a finger to his mouth, signaling me not to speak. I observe his face up close and notice that he is fascinating, mysterious, and extremely handsome. I am jolted when he places his perfect fingers on my lips and traces a circle. He does it gently, my lips are moist, and almost spontaneously I draw closer to the bars, pressing my face against them. His eyes brighten, but he is absolutely, eternally calm. His fingers enter deeply into my mouth, lubricated by my saliva.

Then he withdraws them, and with the aid of his other hand, he rips open the upper part of my threadbare clothes, leaving my full breasts exposed. The nipples are rigid from the cold entering the narrow embrasure, and at the touch of his soaked fingers, they become even harder. He places his lips on my breasts, nuzzling them at first, then kissing them. I hang back my head in pleasure, but my chest remains still, yielding only to his demands. He stops, gazes at me, smiles. One of his hands searches through his clothes, which, from up close, I realize are those of a clergyman.

A jingling of keys, followed by the sound of an iron-clad

door softly closing. He is inside. With me. He again tears at
my clothes, ripping them from my body, exposing my belly
and then, farther below, my warmest point. He slowly lays
me down on the floor. His head descends, and his tongue
thrusts between my legs. While I am no longer cold, I desire
to feel myself, to perceive myself through him. I pull him
toward me, smelling my humours on his face. Groping
beneath his tunic, I feel his member in my hand, lovely and
hard, and I rub it more and more frenetically... His penis
wants to escape from the tunic, and I help it by lifting the
black garment.

He penetrates me, our fluids run together, and he slides
wonderfully, like a knife in warm butter, but he does not
stir me. He slips his member out and sits in a corner. I let
him wait; only later do I approach him. Again he immerses
it in my foaming waves. A few strokes, hard, sharp, sudden,
are enough to bring me to infinite pleasure. We are in
unison. He regains his composure and abandons me,
weeping even more than I was before.

Then I open my eyes, and I am back at the airport,
observing my face.

A dream within a dream. A dream that echoes what
happened yesterday. His eyes were the same as Germano's.
The fire illuminated them, made them shine. Gianmaria had
entered with two huge logs and some branches. He
arranged them in the fireplace, which began to brighten
the setting, making it more hospitable. A strange,
comforting warmth was invading me. What I observed did
not provoke any feeling of disgust or embarrassment. On
the contrary, it was as if my eyes were accustomed to
certain scenes, and the passion that had beaten against my
skin all this time flew out and struck the faces of the two
young men who unwittingly were in my hands. I watched
each of them plunge into the other: I in an armchair beside
the fire, they on a couch in front of it, lovingly eyeing and

touching each other. Their every moan was an "I love you"; and while in my viscera I experienced every thrust as devastating and painful, for them it was a pure caress. I too wanted to take part in an intimacy I did not understand, in their loving and tender refuge, but I had not proposed it and just watched according to our agreement. I was naked, pure in body and mind. Then Germano shot a blissful glance at me. He detached himself from the cleft and, much to my amazement, knelt before me, slowly prying open my thighs. He awaited a sign from me before he dove into that world. He kept at it for a little while, then went back to being himself, the hard and implacable African King. We exchanged places: he pulled me by the hair and bent me towards his sceptre. That was the moment when I noticed his eyes, when I understood that his passion wasn't any different from mine: they took each other by the hand, grappled, then fused.

The lovers fell asleep on the couch in an embrace while I, my skin incandescent from the flames, continued to watch them, alone.

24 January 2002

The winter weighs me down in every sense. The days are so much the same, so monotonous, that I can't bear them any longer. Wake up very early, go to school, argue with my teachers, come back home, do homework till incredibly late, watch some garbage on TV, read a book for as long as my eyes stay open, then go to sleep. Day after day passes like this, except for the unexpected phone calls from the arrogant angel and his devils. When that happens, I dress as best I can, I take off the clothes worn by the diligent student and put on those of the woman who drives men crazy. I am grateful to them because they give me an opportunity to break away from the dreariness and be something different.

When I'm home, I log onto the Internet. I search, explore. I search for everything that simultaneously excites and sickens me. I search for excitement born from humiliation. I search for annihilation. I search for the most bizarre individuals, people who send me sadomasochistic photos, who treat me like a real whore. People who want to unload: rage, sperm, anguish, fear. I'm no different from them. My eyes take on a sickly light, my heart beats madly. I believe (or perhaps I delude myself?) that in the labyrinthine web I will find someone who is willing to love me. Whoever this might be: man, woman, old, young, married, single, gay, transsexual. Anybody.

Last night I entered a lesbian chat room. To try a woman. I don't find the idea entirely repulsive. More than anything else it embarrasses me, frightens me. Some women have made contact, but I trashed the messages right away, without even looking at the photos.

This morning I found a message from a twenty-year-old girl. She says her name is Letizia, and she too is from Catania. The message says very little, just her name, age, and phone number.

1 February 2002
7:30 pm

At school they offered me a role in the play.

Finally I can spend my days doing something fun. I go on stage in a month or so, at a theatre in the centre of town.

5 February 2002
10:00 pm

I phoned her. Her voice is a bit shrill. Her tone is cheerful, easygoing, unlike mine, which is melancholy, serious. After a little while I loosened up and smiled. I didn't have the slightest desire to hear about her and her life. I was only curious to know her physically. In fact, I asked her, "Excuse me, Letizia, you don't by any chance have a photo you can send me?"

She laughed out loud and exclaimed, "Of course I do! Turn on your computer, and I'll send it immediately, while we're on the phone, so you can tell me it's arrived."

"Great," I said, satisfied.

In the photo she is beautiful, incredibly beautiful. And nude. Inviting, sensual, captivating.

"Is that really you?" I stammered.

"Of course! Who do you think it is?"

"Yes, I believe it's you. You're ... so beautiful," I said, stupefied (and made stupid!) by the photo and my own rapture. I don't really like women. On the street I don't turn around when a beautiful woman passes by, I don't lust for female bodies, and I've never seriously thought of having a relationship with a woman. But Letizia has an angelic face and lovely fleshy lips. Beneath her belly I saw a sweet island where one might land, lush and jagged, fragrant and sensual. And her breasts, like two gentle hillocks topped by two large pink circles.

"And you?" she asked me. "Do you have a photo you can send me?"

"Yes," I said. "Wait a minute."

I chose one I found at random on my hard drive.

"You look like an angel," Letizia said. "You're delightful."

"I may look like an angel," I said with a wink, "but I'm really not."

"Melissa, I want to meet you."

"Likewise," I responded.

After we ended the call, she texted me: "I would cover your neck with burning kisses while my hand explores you . . ."

I removed my panties, slipped beneath the covers, and put an end to the sweet torture that Letizia had unwittingly set in motion.

7 February 2002

Today at Ernesto's I saw Gianmaria again. He was very pleased and gave me a big hug. He said that, thanks to me, things between him and Germano have changed. He didn't go into detail, and I didn't ask. All the same, whatever drove Germano to do what he did that night remains unclear to me. I obviously brought it on. But how? Why? Only I have remained the same, Diary.

8 February
1:18 pm

More searches. They won't ever stop till I've found what I want. But I really don't know what I want. Keep on searching, Melissa, forever.

I entered a chat room called "Perverse Sex", using the nickname "whore". I scrolled through the various preferences and inserted the data that interested me. I was instantly contacted by "the_carnage". He was direct, explicit, invasive, and that's just the way I wanted it.

"How do you like to be screwed?" was his opening line.

"Brutally," I replied. "I want to be treated like an object."

"You want *me* to treat you like an object?"

"I don't want anything. Do what you must do."

"You know you're my whore, right?"

"It's hard for me to belong to someone; I'm not even my own."

He started to explain how and where he would put his cock in me, how long I would want it inside, how much I would enjoy it.

I watched the stream of words being sent faster and faster. My stomach was tied in knots, and inside me throbbed a desire with a life of its own, so seductive that I couldn't do anything but yield. Those words were the sirens' song, and I exposed myself deliberately, yet painfully.

Only after telling me he came in his hand did he ask how old I was.

"Sixteen," I wrote.

He filled the screen with emoticons, smiles of amazement followed by a smiley face. Then: "Fucking aye! *Brava!*"

"For what?"

"You're already such an expert."

"Yes."

"I don't believe it."

"What do you want me to say? It doesn't matter anyway; we'll never meet. You're not even in Catania."

"Oh, but I *am* in Catania."

Shit! What horrible luck to be contacted by a Catanian!

"What do you want from me now?" I asked him, certain of his response.

"I want to screw you."

"You just did."

"No." Another smiley face. "For real."

I thought about it for a few seconds, then keyed in the number of my cell. Just when I was about to send it, I hesitated a moment. His "*Grazie!*" made me realize what an idiotic thing I'd just done.

I don't know anything about him, only that his name is Fabrizio and he's thirty-five.

We're meeting in Corso Italia in half an hour.

9:00 pm

I'm well aware that the devil sometimes sails under false colours, revealing his identity only after he has defeated you. First he looks at you with sparkling green eyes, then smiles kindly, gives you a gentle kiss on the neck, and then swallows you whole.

The man who appeared before me was elegant but not quite handsome: tall, robust, thinning salt-and-pepper hair (who knows if he was really thirty-five), green eyes, and grey teeth.

At first sight I was charmed, but then the realization that this was the man from the chat room made me tremble. We strolled the clean sidewalks that fronted the chic shops with their gleaming windows. He talked to me about himself, his job, the wife he never loved but married nevertheless for the sake of their child. He has a fine voice, but a stupid laugh that really annoys me.

While we were walking, he wrapped an arm around me and squeezed my breast. I gave him a polite smile, irritated by his intrusiveness and worried about what would happen next.

I could have left, of course, taken off on my scooter and returned home to watch my mother knead the dough for the *torta di mele*, or listen to my sister read aloud, or play with the cat... I can enjoy normalcy and thrive within its boundaries – I can beam when I get a good grade in school, smile bashfully when I receive a compliment. But nothing amazes me, everything is empty and hollow, vain, lacking susbtance, bland.

I followed him to his car, which took us straight to a garage. The ceiling was damp, and the small space was cluttered with boxes and tools.

Fabrizio threw himself on top of me, but fortunately I didn't feel the full weight of his body. He penetrated me slowly, gently. He wanted to kiss me, but I turned my head. No one has kissed me since Daniele. The heat of my sighs I reserve for my reflected image; and although the softness of my lips has too often touched the thirsty members of the arrogant angel and his devils, they have never, I'm certain, savoured that softness. So I shifted my head to avoid contact with his lips, but I gave him no hint of my disgust. I pretended I merely wanted to change position. He, like an animal, transformed the gentleness that had first surprised me into crude bestiality, grunting and shouting out my name as his fingers pressed into my hips.

"I'm here," I told him. The situation seemed grotesque to me. I didn't understand why he was uttering my name, but to remain insensible to his calls felt embarrassing, so I reassured him, saying, "I'm here," and he calmed down a little.

"Let me come inside you," he said, crazed with pleasure, "come on, please, let me come inside."

"No, you can't."

He suddenly pulled out, voicing my name more loudly till it gradually became a faint echo, a long final sigh. Then, not satisfied, he came at me again, once more I had him inside, his tongue touched me fleetingly, heedless. My pleasure hadn't arrived and yet his returned, a futile thing that had no regard for me.

"Your cunt lips are so big and juicy I could just bite them. Why don't you shave? You'd be even more beautiful."

I didn't respond: what I do with it is none of his business.

A car noise gave us a start. We quickly got dressed (I

couldn't wait). He caressed my chin and said, "The next time, little one, we'll be more comfortable."

I climbed out of the car, its windows fogged, and everyone in the street noticed that my hair was mussed and I was upset, leaving a driver who had salt-and-pepper hair and a crooked tie.

11 February

Things aren't going so well at school. It may be because I'm lazy and scattered, or because the teachers are too reductive and dogmatic... Perhaps I have a somewhat idealistic vision of school and teaching in general, but the reality utterly disappoints me. I hate maths! The fact that it isn't a matter of opinion makes me angry. And then there's that idiot of a teacher who keeps calling me a know-nothing without being able to explain anything! In *Il Mercatino* I pored over the classified ads in search of tutors and found a couple of interesting possibilities. Only one was available. A man; from the sound of his voice he seems rather young. Tomorrow we'll meet to sort things out.

Letizia throbs in my brain from morning to night; I don't know what's happening to me. Sometimes I feel like I'm up for anything.

10:40 pm

Fabrizio called me, and we talked a long time. At the end, he asked me if I had access to a place where we might meet. I answered no.

"Then the time has come," he said, "to give you a splendid gift."

12 February

The maths tutor opened the door in a white shirt and black boxers, wet hair and tortoiseshell glasses. I bit my lip and said hello. His greeting was a smile, "Please, Melissa, make yourself comfortable." I felt the same sensation as when I was a child and mixed milk, oranges, chocolate, coffee, and strawberries in the space of an hour. He shouted to someone in the next room, saying that he was going into the bedroom with me. He opened the door, and for the first time I entered the bedroom of a normal man: no pornographic photos, no imbecilic trophies, no clutter. The walls were covered with old photos, posters of old heavy metal groups, Impressionist prints. And there was an unusual, seductive fragrance that went right to my head.

He didn't excuse his obviously informal attire, and I thought it rather amusing that he didn't. He asked me to sit on the bed while he took the chair at the desk and drew it closer, placing it in front of me. I felt a bit awkward...damn! I was expecting some dry-as-dust pedagogue in a canary yellow V-neck sweater, with his hair combed forward and dyed the same shade as the sweater. Instead I found myself before a tanned, sweet-scented, and extremely attractive young man. I still hadn't removed my overcoat, and with a laugh he said, "Hey, watch I don't eat you when you take that off."

I laughed as well, displeased by the fact that he couldn't eat me. I hadn't yet registered his shoes: no white socks, fortunately, just a slender ankle and a tanned, well-groomed foot that made concentric movements while we discussed the fee, the syllabus, and the schedule for our lessons.

"We're going to start at the very beginning," I said.

"Don't worry: I'll have you start at the two times table." He winked.

I was seated on the edge of the bed with my legs crossed

and my hands folded on my knee.

"You have such a lovely way of sitting." He interrupted me as I was talking about my maths teacher.

I bit my lip again and snorted as if to say, "Do you really expect me to take you seriously? What a cheesy line!"

"Ah, I nearly forgot," he said, changing the subject. "My name is Valerio. Don't ever call me Professor; you'll make me feel too old." He shook his finger in a mock threat.

I dallied a little: after so many witty remarks on his part, I obviously had to make one.

I cleared my throat and said softly, "What if I really wanted to call you Professor?"

This time it was he who bit his lip. He shook his head and asked, "And why would you want to do that?"

I shrugged and after a brief pause said, "Because it's more fun, is it not, Professor?"

"Call me whatever you like, just don't look at me with those eyes," he said, visibly disturbed.

Here I go again, the same old same old. What can I possibly do about it? I can't avoid arousing someone I find attractive, sitting so close to me. I score a bull's eye with every word, every break in the conversation, and I feel great. It's a game.

18 February
8:35 pm

They're already eating supper in the kitchen. I've stolen a moment to write, because I really want to take stock of what happened.

Today I had my first lesson with Valerio. I managed to learn something with him, perhaps because I love to gaze at his

shoulders and his elegant, tapering fingers as they accompany
the movements of the pen. I was able to solve two problems,
even if it was a struggle. He was very serious, professional, and
this made him more attractive. He has captured me. The looks
he sent me were awestruck, and yet he sought to maintain a
discreet distance between us – lest my cunning interfere with
his teaching.

I wore a tight skirt for the occasion; I wanted to seduce
him brazenly. So, when I stood up and headed for the door,
he started to walk behind me, almost brushing against me.
To play with him, I alternated quick strides with slower
steps in such a way that he was forced to come close and
then immediately back off.

When I pressed the button for the elevator, I felt his
breath on my neck, and in a whisper he said, "Keep your
phone free tomorrow night between 10 and 10:15."

19 February 2002
10:30 pm

Two bits of news (as usual, one good, one bad).

Fabrizio has bought a little apartment downtown where
we can see each other without being discovered by our
respective families.

On the phone he was all peachy: "I've had a gigantic screen
mounted in the bedroom so we can watch some of those
flicks, eh, little one? You'll have your own set of keys, of
course. A big kiss on your lovely little face. *Ciao, ciao.*"

This is obviously the bad news.

He didn't give me any time to respond, to make him
aware of my uncertainties, my misgivings. What he's done
seems so rash to me. I had intended to go to bed with him

one more time and then *arrivederci* and *grazie*. I don't want to become the lover of some married man with a daughter to support! I don't want him, his apartment, his gigantic screen for porno films; I don't want him to buy my complaisance as if he were buying his high-tech gadgets. I've suffered enough with Daniele and the arrogant angel, and now, just as I'm restarting my life on my own terms, this fat, necktie-wearing ogre comes along and tells me he wants to commit himself sexually to me. Yet punishment always hovers over our heads, the sharpened point of the sword is poised there, ready to pierce our skulls when we least expect it. The sword will strike him as well, because I shall seize the hilt.

Now for the good news.

The phone call arrived and ended punctually.

I was naked, sitting on the floor, my skin touching the cold marble in my room. As I held the phone, the voice I longed to hear reached me fluid and sensual. He told me one of his fantasies. We were in a classroom, and I was following one of his lessons. At a certain point, I asked him if I could go to the bathroom, and on my way out I gave him a note that contained two words: "Follow me." I was waiting for him in the bathroom; when he arrived, he ripped open my blouse. With the tip of his finger, he gathered some of the drops that dribbled from the tap in the sink and dabbed them on my chest, where they slowly trickled down. Then he lifted my short pleated skirt and penetrated me, as I leaned against the wall and gathered his pleasure into my viscera. The droplets were still trickling down my body, wetting it, leaving thin trails on my skin. We regained our composure and returned to the classroom, where from the first row I followed the chalk flowing across the blackboard in the same way that he was flowing inside me.

We touched ourselves while on the phone. My sex was swollen as never before, and Lethe was flooding the Secret in waves. My fingers were impregnated with me, but also with

him, I felt him close by, despite the circumstances, I felt his
warmth, smelled his scent, imagined his taste.

At 10:15 he said, "Good night, Lo."

"Good night, Professor."

20 February 2002

There are days when I don't know whether to stop
breathing once and for all or to suffer recurrent attacks of
apnoea for the rest of my life. Days when I breathe beneath
the covers and gulp down my tears and discern their taste
on my tongue. I awake with my bed a mess, my hair
unkempt, my skin violated. Naked, before the mirror, I
examine my body. I perceive a tear fall from my eye to my
cheek; I wipe it away with a finger and scratch myself
slightly on the jaw with a fingernail. I pass my hands
through my hair, draw it back, pull a face, just to be likable
to myself, to laugh at myself. But I don't succeed, I want to
cry, I want to punish myself.

I head for the top drawer of the dresser. First I scrutinize
everything inside it, then carefully select what I must wear. I
place all the garments on the bed, folded, and shift the
mirror to a position that faces me. I again examine my body.
The muscles are still taut, although the skin is soft and
smooth, pure white like a baby's. And I am a baby. I sit on
the edge of the bed and slip into the stockings, pointing my
foot, sliding the thin veil over the skin till the lace band
reaches the thigh, exerting a slight pressure. Then it's time
for the corset, black silk with lace and ribbons. It encircles
my bust and tapers my waist, which is already quite thin,
accentuating my hips even more, making them too shapely,
too curvaceous and buttery for men to refrain from releasing
their bestiality there. The breasts are still small: they are firm,

white, round; they can fit in a hand and warm it with their heat. The corset is tight, the breasts are squeezed close together. This still isn't the moment to examine myself. I put on shoes with stiletto heels, slipping in the foot as far as the ankle, and I feel my short stature suddenly gain a few inches. I go to the bathroom, take the red lipstick, and colour my soft, succulent lips; then I thicken the eyelashes with mascara, comb the long, sleek hair, and spray the perfume that sits above the mirror, three times. I return to my room. There I shall see the person who thrills me deeply, body and soul. I examine myself, enchanted, eyes glistening, nearly in tears. A special light sketches the contour of my body, and my hair falling gently on my shoulders invites my caress. The hand falls slowly from the hair, toward the neck, almost unawares; it caresses the delicate skin, and two fingers encompass the circumference, pressing gently. I hear the sound of pleasure, still virtually imperceptible. The hand descends a bit farther and begins to caress the smooth hair. The baby attired as a woman appears before me. Her eyes burn with desire (for what? sex? love? real life?). The baby is sole mistress of herself. Her fingers slip into the folds of her sex, and the heat makes a shudder rise to her head. A thousand sensations invade me.

"You're mine," I murmur, and at once the excitement takes over my desire.

I bite my lip with perfect white teeth, the dishevelled hair makes my back sweat, pearly beads adorn my body.

I pant, the sighs increase... I close my eyes, my body ripples with spasms, my mind is free and takes wing. My knees buckle, my breathing is laboured, my tongue passes wearily over my lips. I open my eyes and smile at the baby. I draw close to the mirror and offer her a long, intense kiss. My breath fogs the glass.

I feel alone, abandoned. I feel like a planet around which three different stars are now orbiting: Letizia, Fabrizio, and the Professor. Three stars keep me company in my thoughts, but not in reality.

21 February

I accompanied my mother to the veterinarian to have my kitten examined. He suffers from a slight case of asthma. He meowed softly, frightened by the doctor's gloved hands; I caressed his head, consoling him with sweet words.

In the car my mother asked me how school was going and what was happening with the boys. I gave vague responses to both questions. At this point, I ordinarily lie; it would feel strange if I stopped.

I asked her to come with me to my maths tutor's house, since it was time for a lesson.

"I'd be delighted. I'm finally getting to meet him!" she said with enthuasiasm.

I didn't respond because I didn't want her to suspect anything. Besides, I was certain that Valerio was expecting to meet my mother sooner or later.

This time, fortunately, his clothes were more presentable, but strangely, when my mother asked me to escort her back to the elevator, she said, "I don't like him. He's got the face of a pervert."

I gestured dismissively and told her he'd only be giving me maths lessons, we weren't going to get married. My mother has this obsession about knowing people from their faces; it's something that really gets on my nerves!

Once the door was closed, Valerio hurried me to get my notebook and start immediately. We didn't say a word about the phone call, nothing but cubes, squares, binomials . . . His eyes were so impenetrable as to leave me in doubt. What if he made that phone call just to mock me? What if I didn't matter at all to him, if he just wanted an orgasm over the phone? I was expecting some sign, a brief exchange, something!

Then, while he was handing me the notebook, he looked at me as if he had understood everything and said, "Don't make any plans for Saturday night. And don't get dressed till I call you."

I stared at him, astonished, but I didn't say anything. Trying to feign an absurd indifference to his words, I opened the notebook and saw what he had written. Amid the x's and y's in tiny letters I read:

> *I still dwelled deep in my elected paradise – a paradise whose skies were the colour of hell-flames – but still a paradise.*
> Professor Humbert

Once more I did not speak. We said goodbye, and he reminded me again about the appointment. As if I could ever forget about it . . .

22 February

At one pm I received a call from Letizia, who asked me if I wanted to have lunch with her. I answered yes, partly because I didn't have enough time to return home: the rehearsal for the play would begin at 3:30. I longed to see her; at night I often thought about her before going to sleep.

In person she was even more beautiful, more real. I watched her soft hands pour the wine and then immediately examined mine which, thanks to the cold I brave every morning on the scooter, had turned red and chapped like an ape's.

She talked to me about everything; in an hour she managed to tell me her entire life. She talked about her family: her mother, who had died prematurely; her father, who had emigrated to Germany; and her sister, whom she rarely sees since her marriage. She told me about her teachers, her years at school and the university, her hobbies, her job.

I gazed at her eyebrows and was overwhelmed with the desire to kiss her. Eyebrows are such bizarre things! Letizia's move with her eyes and are so lovely as to induce you to kiss their perfection, then descend to her face, her cheeks, her mouth... Now, Diary, I do know I desire her. I desire her warmth, her skin, her hands, her saliva, her whispery voice. I would like to caress her head, visit her island and breathe in its air, thrill every inch of her body. And yet I obviously feel blocked, it's such a new thing for me, and I certainly can't pretend that she is experiencing the same sensations, or perhaps she does have them but I'll never know. She looked at me and moistened her lips; her look was ironic, and I felt myself surrender. Not to her, but to my whims.

"Do you want to make love, Melissa?" she asked me as I sipped some wine.

I placed my glass on the table, looked at her, unsettled, and nodded my assent.

"But you'll have to teach me."

Teach me how to make love with a woman or teach me how to love? Perhaps the two things compensate for each other...

23 February
5:45 am

Saturday night or, better, Sunday morning, since the night has already passed, and the sky has brightened. I feel happy,

Diary: my body is saturated with such euphoria, although becalmed by a sensation of utter bliss; a sweet, unbroken tranquillity engulfs me completely. Tonight I learned that letting yourself go with someone you like, someone who overwhelms your senses, is a sacred thing. It's then that sex ceases to be merely sex and begins to be love, while nuzzling the scented skin on his back or caressing his strong, soft shoulders or smoothing his hair.

Not for nothing was I agitated: I knew what I was about to do. I knew I was deceiving my parents. I was getting into a car with a twenty-seven-year-old guy I scarcely knew, an attractive maths teacher, someone who inflamed my senses. I waited for him outside the house, beneath the awesome pine tree, and I saw his green car slowly approach. He wore a scarf around his neck, and the reflection from his glasses thrilled me. Contrary to what he said a few days ago, I didn't wait for him to instruct me on what I should wear. I chose the lingerie from the top drawer, put it on, and then donned a little black dress. I looked at myself in the mirror and pulled a face, thinking I was missing something. I slipped my hands under the dress and slid down my panties. I smiled, whispered, "Now you're perfect," and blew myself a kiss.

When I left the house, I felt the cold seep under the dress, and the surly wind grazed my bare sex. After I'd got into the car, the Professor looked at me with bright, enchanted eyes and said to me, "You didn't put on what I asked you to wear."

I directed my gaze toward the road before me and replied, "I know: disobeying teachers is what I do best."

He gave me a slightly noisy kiss on the cheek, and we set off for a secret place.

I kept running my fingers through my hair. He may have thought it was tension, but it was really desire. The desire to have him there, at once, without any preliminaries. I don't know what we talked about during the journey because my mind was fixated on the thought of possessing him. I looked at his eyes as he drove. I like his eyes: they're intriguing, magnetic, with long, black lashes. I noticed that he cast furtive glances at me, but I acted as if nothing were happening. Then we arrived at Paradiso, or perhaps the Inferno, depending on your point of view. His car continued down deserted, narrow streets that seemed impossible to navigate. We passed a dilapidated church covered with ivy and moss, and Valerio told me, "Keep an eye on your left: you'll see a fountain; the next turn is the place."

I peered down the street, hoping to spot the fountain inside the dark labyrinth.

"There it is!" I exclaimed a little too loudly.

He switched off the engine before a rusty green gate, and the headlights illuminated some words written on it. My eyes rested on two names inserted in a heart so shakily drawn that it seemed to be quivering: Valerio and Melissa.

I looked at him, stunned, and pointed out what I read.

He smiled and said, "I can't believe it!" Then he turned toward me and whispered, "You see? We're written in the stars."

I didn't understand what he meant. Nonetheless, the "we" reassured me and made me feel part of a team where the members were matched instead of mismatched like me and the mirror.

I was afraid of this paradise: it was dark, steep, almost unattainable, especially since I was wearing boots with very high heels. I tried to catch hold of him as fast as possible; I wanted to feel his warmth. We kept on stumbling over stones. On those dark, narrow, walled-in streets the only visible thing was the sky, tonight dense with stars, and the moon coming and going, playing just as we were. I don't know why, but this place filled me with gloomy, macabre sensations. Stupidly, or perhaps legitimately, I thought that somewhere nearby a black mass was unfolding, and I was the designated victim. Hooded

men would bind me to a table, I would be surrounded by
candles and candelabra, they would rape me one by one and
finally kill me, using a dagger with a sharp, sinuous blade. But
I trusted him; perhaps these thoughts were due to my
absorption in the magic of the moment.

The alley that provoked such fears led us to a clearing
that juts out over the sea. You could hear the waves foaming
on the shore. There were huge rocks, white and smooth: I
immediately imagined the purpose they could serve. As we
approached each other, we stumbled yet again. He pulled me
closer to him, drawing me to his face. Our lips grazed
without kissing, as we inhaled our scents and listened to our
breathing. We joined and devoured our lips, sucking and
biting them. Our tongues met: his was hot and soft; it
caressed my mouth like a feather, making me tremble. The
kisses turned red-hot till he asked if he could touch me, if it
was time. Yes, I replied, now's the time. When he discovered I
wasn't wearing panties, he froze, and for a few seconds he
remained motionless before my bare flesh. Then I noticed
his pressure, as he began to massage my erupting volcano.
He told me he wanted to taste me.

I sat on one of the enormous rocks, and his tongue
caressed my sex as a mother's hand caresses a newborn's
cheek: slowly, gently. The pleasure I experienced was
continuous, relentless, dense and fragile at the same time. I
was melting.

He rose and kissed me, and I tasted my juices on his
mouth, and they tasted sweet. I had already brushed against
his member numerous times and felt it hard and meaty
beneath his jeans. I unbuttoned them, and he offered me his
penis. I'd never been with a circumcised man before; I didn't
know the glans would already be exposed. It was like a
velvet tip, smooth and soft, and I couldn't help but approach
it.

I rose, and drawing close to his ear, I whispered, "Fuck me."

He too wanted it, and as I was rising from my kneeling position, he asked me where I had learned to give head like that. My serpentine tongue had driven him crazy.

He asked me to lie face down against the rock, my buttocks in full view. Then he examined them, a bizarre gesture to my mind, yet sensing his gaze upon my curves really excited me. I awaited the first thrust, my hands placed on the cold, smooth stone. He approached and aimed for the target. I wanted him to tell me how I was offering myself to him: a little slut who never gets enough. I uttered a moan of assent that accompanied an abrupt, well-positioned thrust. Then I separated myself from that pleasing puzzle, and gazing at him imploringly, wanting to feel him inside me again, I told him that pausing a few minutes would intensify our pleasures.

"Let's go back to the car," I said. "We'll be more comfortable there."

We again traversed the dark labyrinth, but this time I wasn't afraid. My body was being traversed by a thousand sprites that delighted in chasing after each other and making me feel by turns distressed and euphoric, ineffably euphoric. Before climbing back into the car, I again observed the names written on the gate and smiled, letting him get inside first. Right away I stripped, completely; I wanted every cell of our bodies, our skin, to touch and share exciting new sensations. I straddled him and began to ride him ardently, alternating gentle, rhythmic thrusts with ones that were abrupt, hard, grinding. As I licked and kissed him, I heard him moan. His moans were killing me, I lost control. It's easy to lose control with him.

"We are two masters," he said at a certain point. "How shall one be forced to submit to the other?"

"Two masters," I answered, "who fuck and take turns enjoying themselves."

I machine-gunned several sharp thrusts, and magically I

seized the very pleasure I thought no man could ever give me, the pleasure that I alone was able to procure myself. I felt spasms everywhere, in my sex, my legs, my arms, even on my face. My entire body was electrified. He removed his sweater, and I felt his naked, hairy torso, burning hot on my creamy breasts. I rubbed my nipples against that marvellous discovery, caressing it with both hands, making it all mine.

I got off his body, and he told me, "Touch it with your finger."

I did, astonished, and saw his member weep. Instinctively my mouth drew near, and I swallowed the sweetest, most sugary sperm I had ever tasted.

He hugged me for a few moments, and for those moments, which seemed infinite to me, I felt as if I had everything. Then he tenderly rested my head on the seat while I was still naked, curled up and lit by the moon.

My eyes were closed, but still I sensed him staring at me. It didn't feel right for him to lay his eyes upon me all that time. Men are never satisfied with your body; beyond caressing it, kissing it, they want it to be imprinted in their heads, never to be erased. I asked myself what he might be experiencing by looking at my body, asleep and motionless. For me, looking isn't necessary, perceiving is more important, and tonight I perceived him. I tried to repress a laugh when I heard him grumble about being unable to find his lighter. With my eyes still closed and my voice hoarse, I told him I'd seen it fly out of his pocket when he threw his shirt on the front seat. He gave me a sad glance and opened the window, letting in the cold that I had not felt before.

After a long silence, he exhaled some smoke and said, "I've never done anything like that."

I knew what was on his mind. I felt this was the moment for a serious conversation that might either jeopardize or strengthen our dangerous, precarious, and exciting relationship.

I slowly approached him from behind, placing my hand on his back and then my lips on my hand. I waited a bit before speaking, but from the start I knew what I had to say.

"The fact that you've never done it doesn't mean it was wrong."

"Nor right," he said, exhaling more smoke.

"Who cares if it was right or wrong? The important thing is that we felt good, we lived deeply." I bit my lip, aware that a grown man wouldn't listen to such a presumptuous young girl.

Yet he turned around, flicked away his cigarette, and said, "This is why you make me lose my head: you're mature, intelligent, and you have this passion inside you that's utterly boundless."

He's the one, Diary. He recognized it. I mean my passion. On the way back home, he told me we'd better stop seeing each other as teacher and student, he couldn't think of me in that role any longer, and besides he never mixes work with pleasure. I replied that it was fine with me. I kissed him on the cheek and opened the gate, while he waited for me to enter the house.

24 February

This morning I didn't go to school; I was too tired. Anyway the play opens tonight, so I have a good excuse.

Around lunchtime I received a message from Letizia, who said she would come at 9 pm on the dot to watch me. Yes, Letizia . . . yesterday I forgot about her. But how does one conjure up perfection in the midst of perfection? Yesterday I had Valerio, and that was enough for me; today I'm alone, and I'm not enough for myself (why am I not anymore?). I want Letizia.

P.S. That cretin Fabrizio! He'd got it into his head to come see me with his wife! It's a good thing he isn't too cocky. In the end, I convinced him to stay home.

1:50 am

I wasn't especially nervous tonight; in fact, I felt somewhat apathetic, and I couldn't wait for the end. All the other actors were cavorting, out of either fear or excitement. I stood behind the curtain to observe the people arriving, on the lookout for Letizia. I didn't see her, and Aldo, the set designer, called to me, saying we had to start. The house lights went down, and the stage lights went up. I darted from the wings like an arrow shot from a bow, arriving on stage just as the director had always instructed me to do during rehearsals (when I never managed to do it). Eliza Doolittle amazed everyone, even me: my speech and gestures were so natural, absolutely fresh. I was thrilled. From the stage I tried to spot Letizia, but no luck. So I waited for the performance to end, along with the cheers and applause, and from behind the now closed curtain I continued to scrutinize the audience in an effort to pick out her face. My parents were there, starry-eyed, clapping loudly; so was Alessandra, whom I hadn't seen for months. Fortunately, there was no sign of Fabrizio.

Then I saw her. Her face was bright and cheerful, and she was clapping like mad. I also like her for her spontaneity, her intense *joie de vivre*; it's exhilarating just to look in her face.

Aldo pulled me by my arm and shouted, "*Brava, brava,* darling! Come on, hurry up, get changed. We're going to celebrate with the others." He had an odd, crazy sort of look; I burst into noisy laughter.

I told him I couldn't, I had to see someone. At that very

moment Letizia arrived with her smile. When she noticed Aldo, her expression changed, her smile vanished, and her eyes darkened. I looked at Aldo and observed the same serious expression descend over his blanched face. I turned around two or three times like an idiot, glancing first at him, then at her, after which I asked: "What is it? What happened?"

They remained silent, gazing at each other with hard, almost threatening eyes.

Aldo spoke first: "It's nothing, nothing, go on. I'll tell the others you can't come. *Ciao, bella.*" He kissed my forehead.

Confused, I watched him as he dashed off. I turned towards Letizia and asked her, "Can I please know what's going on? Do you two know each other?"

She was now more cheerful, but a bit hesitant. She tried to avoid eye contact and lowered her face, covering it with her long, tapering fingers.

Then she looked me straight in the eye and said, "I guess you know Aldo is gay."

We all know it at school; he talks about it openly. I answered yes.

"And?" I tried to get her to continue.

"And, some time ago he was with a guy, and, well, then we met, me and the guy, I mean . . . Right away Aldo suspected something." Her words were slow and fragmented.

"Suspected what?" I asked, simultaneously curious and on edge.

She looked at me with her huge, shining eyes. "No, I can't tell you, I'm sorry . . . I can't."

She averted her gaze and said, "I'm not only a lesbian."

And what am I? A woman, or not quite, since my birth certificate says I'm still too young. A girl, then, who seeks refuge and love in the arms of a woman. But I'm lying, Diary: I'd never allow my better half to resemble me so much; I must be the only female member of the team. What I see in Letizia, what makes me desire her so boldly, is mainly her body, her carnal essence, but also, I must say, her spirit too. I like all of her, she intrigues me, enchants me; for some time now she has become the protagonist of my many fantasies. Love, what I am forever seeking, seems so far away at times, so different from me.

1 March 2002
11:20 pm

When I left the house today, my father was sitting on the sofa watching TV with a vacant look. He asked me where I was going without any real concern, and I felt a response would be superfluous, since nothing I said to him would have changed the expression on his face. He would have remained supine.

If I had told him "I'm going to the apartment a married man just bought for the express purpose of fucking me," it would have provoked the same effect as "To study at Alessandra's house."

I shut the door softly. I didn't want to disturb his abstract thoughts, so distant from me.

Fabrizio has already provided me with keys to the apartment. He told me to wait for him there, he would arrive after work.

I still hadn't seen it; you can just imagine how much it mattered to me. I parked my scooter in front of the building and entered the dim, deserted lobby.

The voice of the concierge made me jump, and a sudden warmth surprised me. She asked me what I wanted.

"I'm the new tenant," I said loudly, emphasizing each word because I foolishly thought she might be deaf. In fact, she immediately explained, "I'm not deaf. Which floor are you on?"

I gave it a moment's thought and said, "The second, the apartment that Signor Laudiani just bought."

She smiled and said, "Ah, yes! Your father told me you should lock the door once you're inside."

My father? I let it slide. It was pointless to explain that he wasn't my father, apart from the obvious embarrassment it would entail.

I opened the door, and as soon as the key clicked, the stupidity and senselessness of what I was about to do really hit me. It was stupid to start something I absolutely did not want. With his dim-witted voice full of enthusiasm, Fabrizio had told me this afternoon would be special, we would inaugurate "our love nest" with something memorable. The last time I did something that somebody had called memorable I sucked five cocks in a dark room reeking of grass. I hoped that today at least the theme would be different. The entrance was small and quite dull: a red carpet gave it a bit of colour. From there I could see all the other rooms, but only in snatches: the bedroom, a tiny living room, a kitchenette, and a utility closet. I avoided going into the bedroom so I wouldn't see what that simpleton had hung on the wall. Instead I headed for the living room. Passing the closet, I couldn't help but notice three coloured boxes stacked on the floor, so I switched on the light and went in. On top of the boxes was a note written in big letters: open the boxes and wear one of the things inside. I was definitely snared; my curiosity was piqued.

I rummaged through them, and, all in all, I must admit that he showed some imagination. In the first box was lingerie, pure white and lacy: a sheer slip, panties that were at once sensual and chaste, a push-up bra. Another note placed inside said, for a baby who needs to be cuddled. First box rejected.

The second box contained a pink G-string with some feathers attached behind it, quite like a rabbit's tail, a pair of fishnet stockings, pink shoes with vertiginous high heels, and another note: for a bunny who wants to be captured by the hunter. Before rejecting it, I wanted to see what the third box would yield.

I liked this game, this unveiling of his desires.

The third box is what I chose: a shiny black body suit in latex, accompanied by long high-heeled leather boots, a whip, a black dildo, and a tube of Vaseline. Apart from some cosmetics, the box also contained a note that read, for a mistress who wants to punish her slave. There could be no punishment better than this; he himself had proposed the means. Below the note was the postscript: if you decide to wear this, you should call me only after you put it on. I didn't understand why he made this request, but it was fine with me, the game was becoming more interesting. I'd make him come and go as I pleased – perfect!

I could tell him to shove it up his asshole without any remorse or guilt. But I was annoyed that I had to play this intriguing game with him. He didn't rank high in my estimation; it would have been fantastic to have all these opportunities with the Professor. But I had to play: he'd done too much to ensure a few fucks with me, first the apartment, now these gifts. I saw my phone flashing; he was calling me. I didn't answer; instead, I texted him that I had chosen the third box and would call him later.

I went into the living room, opened the window that gave onto the balcony, and let in a little fresh air to get rid of the musty smell. Then I lay down on the carpet with the warm, enveloping colours. The fresh air, the silence, the diffuse light coming from the setting sun was lulling me to sleep. I closed my eyes and breathed deeply till I perceived my breathing as a wave ebbing and flowing, breaking on the reef, and then withdrawing again into the vastness of the sea.

A dream was rocking me, and passion held me in its arms. I didn't manage to make out the man, although I knew very well who he might be. His identity escaped me; his features were indistinct. We were fitted together like a key in a lock, like a farmer's spade thrust into the rich, luxuriant soil. His erect member, after nodding off a little while, again began to thrill me with the same shudders as before, and my broken voice showed him how much I was enjoying the game. My desire was making him sluggish, as if I were a cool, fizzy spumante that packed the necessary punch to exalt his senses and send him high as a kite.

He felt increasingly exhausted by my body and my movements, which were rapid and yet slow enough to make him lose any sense of time. I slowly detached my buttocks from his sex so that the arrow did not abruptly leave the open, vermilion wound. Then I observed him with my Lolita smile. I seized the silk garters that had just bound my wrists, this time to tie his. His closed eyes signalled a desire to possess me hard and violent, but I felt I wanted to wait . . . and wait . . .

I then took my black stockings, the thigh-highs with the lace band, and tied his ankles to two chairs I had moved to the edge of the bed. Now he was open to pleasure, his and mine. In the midst of that naked body rose the staff of love, so erect, confident, and inflexible that it did not take long to master my pink secret once again. I climbed up on top of him, rubbed my skin against his, sensing our mutual shudders, driven by gentle waves of pleasure. My rigid nipples lightly caressed his torso, its hair pricking my smooth skin, and his hot breath met mine.

I passed the tips of my fingers over his lips, slowly massaging them; then my fingers entered his mouth, gently, smoothly . . . His moaning made me realize how exciting fingers might be in their journey of discovery. I placed a finger on my dripping rose, moistening it with dew, and then placed it on the coral tip of his stiff penis, which at the touch vibrated slightly in the air like the flag of a commander victorious in battle. Astride him, my buttocks turned toward the mirror and thus reflected in his eyes, I lowered my bosom and whispered "I want you" in his ear.

It was divine to see him at the mercy of my desires, stretched out naked on white sheets that received the outline of his tense, excited body. I took the scented scarf I was wearing when I entered the house, and I blindfolded him so that he could not glimpse the body I permitted him to serve.

I left him there quite a while. Too long. I was crazed with lust, I wanted to straddle that perennially erect shaft, and yet I also wanted to make him wait longer, to wait forever. Finally I rose from the kitchen chair to return to the bedroom where, bound, he was expecting me. He could hear my steps, deliberately quiet and stealthy, and he emitted a sigh of gratitude. He jerked before my body slowly swallowed him up inside it...

I awoke. The sky was an intense blue, and the moon was already visible, attached like a thin hook to the roof of the world. I was still excited by the dream. I picked up my phone and called him.

"I was beginning to think you weren't going to call," he said, worried.

"I did what I felt like," was my nasty reply.

He told me he would arrive in fifteen minutes, and I should wait for him in bed.

I stripped and left my clothes on the floor of the closet. I took the contents of the box and put on the tight body suit, which clung to my back and pulled my skin, pinching it. The boots reached exactly to the middle of my thigh. I didn't really understand why he had also included flaming red lipstick, false eyelashes, and very bright rouge. I went into the bedroom to look at myself in the mirror, and when

I saw my image, I had a start: here was my nth
transformation, my nth prostration to the hidden, prohibited
desires of someone who isn't me and doesn't love me. But
this time would be different; I would exact a fitting
recompense: his humiliation. Even if, in reality, we were both
humiliated. He arrived slightly later than he told me he
would. His excuse was that he had to invent some cock-
and-bull story for his wife. His poor wife, I thought, but
tonight he will be punished for his sins against her as well.

He found me on the bed, intently watching a bluebottle
that was bashing against the light on the ceiling, producing
an irritating noise. I was thinking that people bash
convulsively against the world just like that stupid insect:
they create noise and confusion, they buzz around things
without ever managing to seize them completely; sometimes
they mistake a trap for the object of their desire and get
killed, rotting beneath the blue reflector inside the cage.

Fabrizio placed his overnight bag on the floor and
remained motionless, observing me in silence. His eyes spoke
eloquently, and the excitement beneath his trousers
confirmed everything: I would have to torture him slowly,
maliciously.

Then he said, "You've already raped my head; you've
penetrated me. Now you must rape my body; you must
penetrate my flesh with some part of you."

"Don't you feel that at this point master and slave can no
longer be distinguished? I decide what I must do; you must
only suffer. Come!" I shouted like a most capable
dominatrix.

He headed toward the bed with long, hurried strides.
Eyeing the whip and the dildo on the bedside table, I felt
my blood boil and a frenzied excitement building within
me. I wanted to know what kind of orgasm he would
experience, and above all I wanted to see his blood.

Naked, he looked like a worm, virtually hairless, his skin

bright and soft, his belly flabby and swollen, his sex
unexpectedly stiff. I think that to inflict on him the same
sweet violence as in the dream would have been too much;
he merited a punishment that was harsh, stern, wicked. I
made him stretch out on the floor, on his stomach. The
expression on my face was cold and disdainful, aloof; had he
seen it, his blood would have frozen in his veins. He turned
around his pale, sweaty face, and I ground the heel of my
boot into his back. His flesh was scourged to fulfil my
vendetta. He screamed, but screamed softly; perhaps he wept.
My mind was in such a confused state that it was impossible
for me to distinguish the sounds and colours around me.

"Who are you?" I asked him with an icy tone.

A prolonged wheeze, then a broken voice: "Yours. I am
your slave."

As he spoke, my heel descended along his spine and
rested between his buttocks, pressing.

"No, Melissa . . . No," he said, panting loudly.

I wasn't capable of continuing, so I reached a hand toward
the table, gathered the accessories, and placed them on the
bed. I turned him over with a kick, forcing him to assume a
supine position, and gave his chest the same treatment I had
given his back.

"Turn over!" I ordered him again. He turned. I straddled
one of his thighs and, without realizing, started gently
rubbing my sex, restrained by the clinging bodysuit.

"Your cunt is sopping," he said with a sigh. "Let me lick
it."

"No!" I shouted.

His voice snapped, but I managed to hear him as he told
me to continue, to hurt him.

My excitement was growing, filling my soul and flowing
anew from my sex, provoking a mysterious exaltation. I was
subjugating him, and I was happy. Happy for me and happy
for him. For him because it was what he wanted, one of his

greatest desires. For me because it was a means of asserting my person, my body, my soul, my entire self over another person, swallowing him up completely. I was participating in a celebration of my self. Seizing the whip, I passed first the shaft and then the leather strips over his bottom, although without striking it. I gave him a light blow and felt his body shudder and contract. Above us the bluebottle kept on bashing against the light, and before me hung the curtain, pulled by the half-opened window to the point of ripping. A final violent lash to his tortured, reddened back, and then I grabbed the dildo. I had never held one, and I didn't like it. I coated the surface with the sticky gel, my fingers gauging the falsity of the thing, its utter lack of naturalness. It was very different from seeing Gianmaria and Germano slowly enter each other's bodies, doing it gently, tenderly, being inside a reality that was different but true, comforting. The present reality repulsed me: it was completely false, miserably hypocritical. He was hypocritical in relation to his life, his family, a worm who prostrated himself at the feet of a girl. The dildo entered with difficulty, and I felt it vibrate in my hand as if it had split something: his guts. As I was penetrating him, I repeated a series of phrases in my head, like a litany chanted during a rite.

This is for your ignorance: first thrust. This is for your feeble presumptuousness: second thrust. For your daughter who will never know she has a father like you; for your wife who lies next to you at night; for not including me, for not understanding me, for not grasping the fundamental essence of me, which is beauty. That true beauty which we all have, but you lack. I gave him countless thrusts, every one rough, sharp, lacerating. He was groaning beneath me, screaming, weeping at times. His orifice widened, and I saw it red with tension and blood.

"Can't you take it, you disgusting brute?" I sneered cruelly.

He screamed at the top of his voice; perhaps he experienced an orgasm. Then he said, "Enough, I beg you."

And I stopped as my eyes filled with tears. I left him on the bed, ravaged, destroyed, completely broken. I got dressed, and in the lobby I said goodbye to the concierge. I hadn't say goodbye to him, I hadn't looked at him, I just left, and that was it.

When I arrived home, I didn't look in the mirror. Before going to sleep, I gave myself a hundred brush strokes. To see my face destroyed and my hair mussed would have hurt me, too much.

4 March 2002

The night was filled with horrific dreams. One in particular made me quake.

I was running through a dark barren forest chased by mysterious evil characters. Before my eyes rose a tower lit by the sun; it was just like Dante trying to reach the hill but failing because he was thwarted by three wild beasts. Except that I wasn't actually thwarted by three wild beasts, but rather by an arrogant angel and his devils and behind them an ogre with a bellyful of babies' bodies and farther on an androgynous monster followed by young sodomites. They were all foaming at the mouth, and someone was dragging himself laboriously, scraping his body along the parched earth. I was running, turning around constantly for fear that one of them might reach me; they were all screaming incoherent, unpronounceable phrases. At a certain point, I stopped paying attention to the obstacle before me and began shouting. Opening my eyes wide, I spotted the kind face of a man who, taking me by the hand, led me through dark secret paths to the foot of the high tower. He held up a finger and said,

"Ascend the stairs and never turn around. At the top, you will halt and discover what you sought in vain in the forest."

"Run, before I meet up with them again!" he screamed, violently shaking his head.

"But you are my saviour! I don't need to climb the tower; I have already found you!" This time I was shouting joyfully.

"Run!" he repeated. Then his eyes changed, turning red and ravenous, and he ran off, foaming at the mouth. I stood there, at the foot of the tower, my heart shattered.

22 March 2002

My parents went away for a week and will return tomorrow. For days I've had the house to myself, and I came and went as I pleased. At the beginning, I thought of inviting someone to spend the night with me, perhaps Daniele, who contacted me a couple of days ago, or Roberto, or perhaps I would dare call Germano or Letizia — someone, in other words, who might keep me company. Instead I enjoyed my solitude; I stayed by myself and thought about all the beautiful things that had recently happened to me, as well as the ugly ones.

I know, Diary, I've hurt myself, I've had no respect for me, for my person, which I say I love so much. I'm not so sure I love myself as I once did: a girl who loves herself doesn't let her body be violated by any man whatsoever, without a specific reason and without even any pleasure. I tell you this as a prelude to revealing a secret, a sad secret that I foolishly wanted to hide from you, deluding myself that I'd forget. One night while I was alone, I thought I'd cheer myself up and get a little air, so I went to the pub where I always go, and after a few beers I met a guy who chatted me up, in a way that was neither nice nor courteous. I was drunk, he turned my head, and I gave him free rein. He brought me back to his place, and when he closed the door behind me, I was overwhelmed with fear, a tremendous fear, which my drunkenness enabled me to repress immediately. I asked him to let me go, but he wouldn't, compelling me with his tiny crazed eyes to undress. Frightened, I did it, and then I did everything he ordered me to do. I penetrated myself with a vibrator he thrust into my hand, and I felt the walls of my vagina burn, felt the skin tear. I cried as he offered me his little, flaccid member. He was holding my head, and I couldn't avoid doing what he wanted. He couldn't come; my jaws, even my teeth were aching.

He threw himself on the bed and abruptly fell asleep. Instinctively, I looked in the bedside table and expected to find the money he would've owed a good whore. I went into the bathroom and washed my face without deigning, even for a wretched instant, to glance at my reflected image. I would've seen the monster that everyone wants me to become. I can't allow myself to become that, I can't allow them to want it. I am dirty; only Love, if it exists, can cleanse me again.

28 March

Yesterday I told Valerio what had happened to me the other night. I expected him to say, "I'll come right away," to take me in his arms and cuddle me, to whisper that I mustn't worry about anything, he would be there with me. None of this happened. He told me in a bitter, reproachful tone that I'm stupid, a fool, and it's true that I am – no shit! But it's already enough that I blame myself, I don't want sermons from other people, I just want someone to hug me and make me feel good. This morning he was waiting for me by the school entrance; I would've never imagined such a surprise. He arrived on a motorcycle, his hair blowing in the wind and a pair of sunglasses covering his splendid eyes. I was chatting away in front of a bench where a few of my classmates were sitting. My hair was a mess, my book bag heavy on my shoulder, and my face flushed. When I saw him arrive with his sly, captivating smile, my jaw dropped, and I was tongue-tied for a moment. I quickly said "Excuse me" to my mates and ran into the street to greet him. I threw myself against him in a childish manner; it was spontaneous and said a great deal. He told me he was longing to see me, he missed my smile and my perfume, he thought he'd fallen into some sort of crisis of abstinence from Lolita.

"What are the clones looking at?" he asked me, nodding toward the kids in the piazza.

"Who do you mean?" I asked.

He explained that this was his term for young people who all look identical, each of them a member of the same great, enormous herd. It's their way of distinguishing themselves from the adult world.

"You have a strange way of defining us. Anyway, they're looking at your bike, they're intrigued by you, and they envy me because I'm talking to you. Tomorrow they'll ask me, 'Who was that guy talking to you?'"

"And what will you say?" he asked, certain of my response.

His certainty irritated me, so I said, "I might or might not answer. It depends on who asks and how they ask."

I looked at his tongue wetting his lips, looked at his eyelashes, long and black as a baby's, and his nose, which seems a perfect copy of mine. Then I looked at his penis, which swelled when I drew close and whispered, "I want to be possessed, now, in front of everybody."

He looked at me and smiled, nervously clenching his lips as if to contain his feverish excitement. Then he asked, "Lo, Lo, do you want to drive me crazy?"

I answered yes with a slow nod and flashed a smile.

"Let me smell your perfume, Lo."

I offered him my pure white neck, and he nuzzled it, filling his lungs with my musky vanilla fragrance. "I'm going now, Lo."

He couldn't leave. This time I was ready to play all my cards.

"You want to know what panties I'm wearing today?"

He was about to start the motor, but he stared at me, Shocked, and with his mind befogged, he answered yes.

I hiked up my trousers, unbuttoning them at the top, so he could see that I wasn't wearing panties. He continued to stare at me, searching for a response.

"I often go pantyless. I like it," I told him. "Remember that night we did it the first time?"

"You're driving me crazy."

I drew near his face, keeping a distance that was very close and therefore very dangerous. "Yes," I said, looking straight into his eyes, "that's my intention."

We gazed at each other without saying a word for a long time. He would occasionally shake his head and smile. I again approached his ear and told him, "Rape me tonight."

"No, Lo . . . it's risky," he replied.

"Rape me," I repeated, at once bossy and wicked.

"Where, Mel?"

"The place where we went the first time."

29 March
1:30 am

I climbed out of the car and closed the door, leaving him inside. I set off down those dark, narrow streets, and he

waited a little while before following me. I found myself
alone, crossing the jagged pavement. I heard the noise of the
sea in the distance, then nothing more. I looked at the stars
and felt as if I had to catch their imperceptible sound, beings
that twinkle intermittently. Then the engine and headlights
of his car. I stayed calm; I wanted everything to unfold as I
had planned it: he was the executioner, I the victim. Victim
in body, humiliated and subjugated. But the mind, mine and
his – I command it, I alone. I desire all this; I am mistress of
it. He is a fake master, a master who is my slave, slave to my
desires and whims.

The car pulled up. He switched off the engine and
headlights and climbed out. For a few moments I thought I
was again alone, as I heard nothing . . . There he goes; I heard
him. He was walking at a slow, calm pace, but he was
breathing fast, panting. Unexpectedly, I felt fear. He started
to pursue me more vehemently, he ran toward me and,
seizing my arm, threw me against the wall.

"Signorinas with lovely little asses shouldn't wander
around the streets alone," he said, his tone of voice changing.

With one hand he held my arm, hurting me; with the
other, he pushed my head toward the wall, pressing my face
hard against the rough, muddy surface.

"Stay still," he ordered.

I was waiting for the next move, I was excited but also
frightened, and I asked myself what I would have felt if a
real stranger were violating me, not my sweet Prof. Then I
erased this thought, recalling a few nights ago and all the
violence my soul has endured so many times . . . and I still
wanted violence, violence beyond endurance. I am
accustomed to it; perhaps I can't do without it. It would
seem strange to me if one day gentleness and tenderness
came knocking at my door and asked to enter. Violence kills
me, wears me down, dirties me, and feeds on me, but with
and for it I survive, I feed on it.

He used his free hand to rummage through a trouser pocket. He squeezed my white wrists hard, released me a moment, then used his other hand to grab the object he had taken from his pocket. It was a blindfold. He tied it around the upper part of my face, covering my eyes.

"You're so beautiful," he said. "I'm raising your skirt, whore. Don't speak, and don't scream."

I felt his hand inside my panties, his fingers caressing my sex. Then he gave me a violent slap; I groaned in pain.

"I told you not to make a sound."

"Actually, you told me not to speak or scream. I groaned," I whispered, knowing he would punish me for this.

In fact, he gave me another slap, even more violent. But I didn't make a sound.

"*Brava*, Lo, you're great."

He bowed down, still holding me tightly, and began to kiss my buttocks, on which he had visited so much violence. When he started to lick them slowly, my desire to be possessed grew, I couldn't stop it. I arched my back to make him seize my lust.

In response I received another slap.

"When I say," he ordered.

I could perceive only sounds and his hands on my body. I was deprived of sight and now of total pleasure.

He let go of my wrists and leaned his entire body against me. With both hands he grabbed my breasts, free of any constraint that might impede him. He grabbed them hard, hurting me, squeezing them with fingers that felt like burning pincers.

"Easy," I murmured, scarcely audible.

"No, it'll be the way I say," and he let loose another very violent slap. As he was rolling my skirt up to my hips, he said, "I would've liked to hold out longer, but I can't. You've got me too worked up, and I can't do anything but give in to you."

He plunged a stake into me, penetrating me deeply, filling me completely with his excitement, his uncontrollable passion.

A powerful, shuddering orgasm swept through my body, and I collapsed against the wall, scratching my skin. He held me, and I felt his hot breath on my neck. His panting made me feel good.

I remained so long like that, too long, long enough that I didn't want it ever to end. Returning to the car meant returning to reality, a cold, cruel reality from which escape was inevitable, as I immediately realized. He and I, the marriage of our souls, had to end there; the circumstances won't ever permit either of us to be completely and spiritually inside the other.

On the way back, stuck in the traffic that brings chaos to Catania every night, he looked at me, smiled, and said, "Lo, I love you." He took my hand, lifted it to his mouth, and kissed it. Lo, not Melissa. He loves Lolita; he knows nothing of Melissa.

4 April 2002

Diary,

I'm writing to you from a hotel room; I'm in Spain, in Barcelona. I'm on a school trip, and I'm having lots of fun even if the sour, obtuse teacher looks at me cockeyed when I say I don't want to visit museums, I feel they're a waste of time. I hate visiting a place just to learn about its history. OK, that's important too, but later what good will it be to me? Barcelona is so alive, upbeat, but with an undercurrent of melancholy. It's like a beautiful, fascinating woman with deep, sad eyes that dig into your soul. It's like me. I'd like to wander through the nocturnal streets lined with bars and swarming with all kinds of people, but they're forcing me to spend the nights in discos where, if things go well, I manage to meet someone who hasn't yet got wasted on alcohol. I don't like dancing; it bores me. There's so much noise in my room: someone's jumping on the bed, someone's chugging sangria, someone's puking in the toilet. I'm going now, Giorgio is pulling me by the arm . . .

7 April

The next-to-last day. I don't want to go home. This is my home, I feel comfortable, safe, happy, understood by the Barcelona natives, even though we don't speak the same language. It's a relief not to hear the phone ringing with calls from Fabrizio or Roberto – and I don't have to concoct some excuse for refusing to meet them. It's a relief to be able to talk late with Giorgio without feeling I have to slip into his bed and give him my body.

Where have you ended up, Narcissa, you who loved yourself so much, who smiled so much, who wanted to give as much as she received? Where have you ended up with your dreams, your hopes, your manias, those of life as well as those of death? Where have you ended up, mirror image? Where do I search for you, where do I find you? How can I control you?

4 May 2002

Today Letizia was standing at the school entrance. She came to meet me with her round face framed by huge sunglasses, quite like those I've seen in photos of my mother from the

1970s. She was with two girls who were obviously lesbians.

One is named Wendy. She's my age, but her eyes make her look much older. The other one, Floriana, is slightly younger than Letizia.

"I've been dying to see you," Letizia told me, gazing into my eyes.

"I'm glad you came," I replied. "I've wanted to see you too."

In the meantime people were leaving school and taking seats on the benches in the piazza. Kids were looking at us curiously, whispering and snickering among themselves. The virgins of Sant'Ilario were even more sour, sanctimonious, and stupid than ever: they turned up their noses and rolled their eyes, fixing the pigtails their mommies made for them that morning before coming to school. I thought I caught some of their comments: "Did you see who she's going around with? I always said she was strange."

Letizia seemed to pick up on my uneasiness, so she said, "We're going to have lunch at the centre. Do you want to come?"

"What centre?" I asked.

"Gay-Lesbian. I have the keys. We'll be alone."

I accepted. I started my scooter and Letizia got on behind me, gluing her breasts to my back and breathing on my neck. We laughed a lot on the road. I was constantly weaving in and out because I wasn't used to carrying another person; she kept on sticking out her tongue at the little old ladies, her arms encircling my waist.

When Letizia opened the door, a special world appeared before my eyes. It was only a house, yet a house that didn't belong to anyone in particular, but to the entire gay community. It was furnished with everything and more; the library contained not only books, but also a huge jar filled with condoms. Displayed on a table were gay magazines, fashion magazines, magazines about cars, others about health. A cat wandered through the rooms, rubbing against our legs, and I caressed him as I caress Morino, my beautiful beloved cat (who is here now, curled up on my desk; I hear him breathing).

We were hungry, so Letizia and Floriana proposed going to buy a pizza from the shop on the corner. As they were about to leave, Wendy gave me a cheerful look with a dim-witted smile. She had a peculiar spring in her step; she seemed like some sort of crazed imp. I was afraid to be alone with her, so I went to the door and shouted for Letizia, saying I wanted to keep her company. Wendy interrupted me, trying to get me to stay inside. My friend immediately guessed what was happening and with a smile invited Floriana to go back. While we were waiting for the pizza, we didn't speak much. Then I said, "Shit, my fingers are frozen!"

Letizia looked at me mischievously, but also ironically. "Mmmm," she said, "I'll have to keep that in mind . . ."

While we were walking back, we met a friend of hers named Gianfranco. Everything about him was sweet: his face, his skin, his voice. His infinite gentleness filled me with happiness. He came inside with us, and we sat talking on the sofa while the others set the table. He told me he was a bank clerk, although his outrageous tie seemed in sharp contrast to the sober world of banking. His voice sounded sad, but asking him about it would've seemed too forward. I felt like him. Then he left, and the four of us sat around the table, chattering away and laughing. Or more precisely I was the only one who was chattering, nonstop, as Letizia looked at me, attentive and at times disconcerted when I spoke about some guy I'd been to bed with.

Later on I stood up and went into the garden, which was neat but not well tended. They had planted tall datepalms and strange trees with prickly trunks and huge pink flowers in their foliage. Letizia walked up and hugged me from behind, grazing my neck with a kiss.

I turned around instinctively and met her mouth: hot, soft, extremely yielding. Now I understood why men love to kiss women so much: a woman's mouth is so innocent, pure, whereas the men I've met always leave me with a slimy trail of saliva, coarsely thrusting their tongues into my mouth. Letizia's kiss was different: it was velvety, fresh yet intense at the same time.

"You're the most beautiful woman I've ever had," she told me as she held my face.

"You too," I responded, although I didn't know why. There was no need to say it since she was my only woman!

Letizia changed roles with me, and this time I took the lead, rubbing my body against hers. I hugged her tightly, breathing her perfume; then she led me to the next room, lowered my pants, and ended the tender torture that had begun a few weeks ago. Her tongue was melting me, but the thought of achieving an orgasm in a woman's mouth made me shudder. While her tongue was licking me, while she was on her knees before me, straining for my pleasure, I closed my eyes, and with my hands folded like the paws of a frightened rabbit, I recalled the invisible little man who used to make love to me in my childhood fantasies. The invisible man is faceless, colourless; he is only a sex and a tongue which I use for my enjoyment. It was then that my orgasm arrived, so powerful it had me panting. Her mouth was full of my sap, and when I opened my eyes, I saw her – what a marvellous surprise – with a hand inside her panties, writhing with the pleasure that was arriving for her too, perhaps more keen and genuine than mine had been.

Later we lay down on the sofa, and I believe I slept for a short while. When the sun set and the sky darkened, she accompanied me to the door, and I told her, "Leti, it would be better if we didn't see each other again."

She nodded, smiled gently, and said, "I agree."

We exchanged a last kiss. When I was heading home on

my motorino, I felt used yet again, used by another and by my own wicked impulses.

18 May 2002

I'm recalling the sound of my mother's warm, reassuring voice. Yesterday, while I was in bed with the flu, she told me this story:

"Something you find difficult, something you don't want, can prove to be a wonderful gift. You know, Melissa, we often receive gifts without our knowledge. This is the story of a young sovereign who assumes the rule of a kingdom. He was beloved before he became king, and his subjects, delighted with his coronation, brought him ever so many gifts. After the ceremony, whilst the new king was dining in his palace, he suddenly heard a knock on the door. The servants found a shabbily dressed old man, to all appearances a beggar, who wished to see the sovereign. They did their utmost to dissuade him, but to no avail. Then the king went to meet him. The old man showered him with praise, telling him that he was very handsome, and that everyone in the kingdom was pleased to have him as sovereign. He had brought the king a gift: a melon. The king detested melons, but to be polite to the old man, he accepted it, thanked him, and the old man departed happily. The king went back inside the palace and handed the fruit to the servants, so that they might toss it into the garden.

"The next week, at the same hour, there was another knock on the door. The king was summoned once again, and the beggar lauded him, offering him another melon. The king accepted it, saluted the old man, and, once again, tossed the melon into the garden. The scene was repeated for several weeks: the king was too polite to affront the old man or to scorn the generosity of his gift.

"Then, one evening, just when the old man was about to deliver the melon to the king, an ape leapt down from a portico and caused the fruit to fall from his hands. The melon broke into a thousand pieces against the façade of the palace. When the king looked, he saw a shower of diamonds fall from the heart of the melon. Anxiously, he ran to the garden behind the palace: all the melons had turned into mounds of jewels."

I stopped her, excited by the beautiful story, and said, "Can I infer the moral?"

She smiled and said, "Of course."

I took a deep breath, just as I do whenever I get ready to repeat a lesson at school. "Sometimes inconvenient situations, problems, or difficulties conceal opportunities for growth; very often in the heart of difficulties shines the light of a precious jewel. It is therefore wise to welcome what is inconvenient and difficult."

She smiled again, stroked my hair, and said, "You've grown, little one. You're a princess."

I wanted to weep, but I restrained myself. My mother didn't know that, for me, the king's diamonds had been the crude bestiality of boorish men incapable of love.

20 May

Today the Prof came to meet me again outside school. I was waiting for him: I gave him a letter in which I enclosed a particular pair of panties.

I am these panties. They describe me best, curiously designed with a dangling ribbon on each side. To whom could they belong, if not some Lolita?

Yet they don't simply belong to me; they are me and my body.

*I happen to have worn them often when I made love,
perhaps never with you, but that doesn't matter. The ribbons
hold back my impulses and my senses; they are the ties that,
apart from leaving a mark on my skin, restrain my feelings.
Imagine my body wearing nothing but these panties. If one
knot is untied, only one of my spirits is released.*

*Sensuality. The spirit of Love is still impeded by the other
knot. Thus, whoever has untied my Sensuality will see only
the woman, the girl, or generically the female, capable of
receiving sex, nothing more. He possesses only half of me, and
it is probably what I want on most occasions. When someone
unties only the knot of Love, I shall give another part of me, a
part that is small but deep. Then the day may come when my
jailer arrives, offering me the keys to release both of my spirits:
Sensuality and Love are set free and take wing. You feel good,
free and satisfied, and your mind and body no longer ask for
anything, no longer torment you with their requests. Like a
tender secret, they are freed by a hand that knows how to
caress you, that knows how to make you throb, and they glow
at the mere thought of that hand.*

*Now smell that part of me which lies exactly in the centre
between Love and Sensuality: it is my Soul, which seeps
through my fluids.*

*You were right when you told me I was born to screw. As
you see, my Soul too wishes to be desired and gives off its
smell, the female smell. Perhaps the hand that freed my spirits
is yours, Prof.*

*I dare say only your sense of smell could fathom my fluids,
my Soul. Don't scold me for saying this, Prof, if I go too far. I
feel I must do it because at least in future I won't regret losing
an opportunity before grasping it. This thing creaks inside me
like a door that needs to be oiled; its noise is deafening. When
we are with you, in your arms, my panties and I are free of
any impediment, any chains. Yet the spirits have met a wall in
their flight, the horrendous and unjust wall of time, which*

passes slowly for one, fast for the other, a series of figures that
keep us at arm's length. I hope your mathematical intelligence
might offer you some hints on how to solve this terrible
equation. But not only this: you recognize only one part of
me, even though you have liberated two. And that isn't the
part I would like to let live on its own. It's up to you to
decide whether to bring about a change in our relationship,
whether to make it become more . . . "spiritual", a tad more
profound. I put my trust in you.
Yours,
Melissa

23 May
3:14 pm

Where is Valerio? Why did he leave me without a kiss?

29 May 2002
2:30 am

I weep, Diary, I weep with immense joy. I've always known
that joy and happiness do exist. This is something I've sought
in so many beds, in so many men, even in a woman,
something I've sought in myself and then forfeited. And now
I've found it in the most anonymous and ordinary of places.
Not in a person, but in a person's eyes. Along with Giorgio
and some others I went to the new café that just opened
right near my house, about fifty metres from the sea. It's an
Arab place with belly dancers who gyrate round the tables
when they're not serving. There are pillows on the floor,
carpets, candles, incense. It was packed, so we decided to

wait till a table was free and we could sit down. I was leaning against a streetlight, thinking about a phone call from Fabrizio. It had ended badly: I told him I didn't want anything from him, and never want to see him again.

He started crying and said he'd given me everything, by which he meant money, money, and more money.

"If this is how you treat people, I don't have to take it. But thanks for the offer, all the same," he shouted ironically. I hung up on him. I didn't answer any more of his calls and won't ever, I swear. I hate that man: he's a worm, a scumbag, I won't give myself to him again.

I was thinking about all this and about Valerio. I was frowning, and my eyes were fixed on some unspecified point. Then, as I was turning away from those irksome thoughts, my gaze met his: who knows how long he was watching me. He was gentle and sweet. I looked at him, and he looked at me, at very brief intervals. We would turn away, but our eyes couldn't help but pounce on each other again. His were deep and sincere, and this time I wasn't deluding myself by creating absurd fantasies about wanting to be hurt or punished. This time I really believed what was happening, I saw his eyes, they were there, staring at me, and they seemed to be saying they wanted to love me, wanted to get to know me better. I began to look more carefully at him. He was sitting with his legs crossed, a cigarette in his hand. His lips were fleshy, his nose slightly pronounced but impressive, and he had the eyes of an Arab prince. He was offering something to me, me alone. He wasn't looking at any other girl, he was looking at me, and not the way men usually look at me on the street, but sincerely and honestly. I don't know what motivated me to do it, but I let out a laugh that was too loud. I couldn't contain myself. I felt so intensely happy I couldn't limit myself to a smile. Giorgio was watching me, amused; he asked me what was up. With a wave I signalled he shouldn't worry and hugged him to justify my sudden explosion. I turned around again and noticed the prince was smiling, offering me a glimpse of his splendid white teeth. It was then that I calmed down and told myself, "Don't forget, Melissa, scare him off. Make him see you're an idiot, a defective, an ignoramus. And above all do it now: don't make him wait!"

While I was thinking this, a girl passed by him and stroked his hair. He looked at her for no more than an instant, then shifted over a bit to get a better look at me.

Giorgio distracted me: "Meli, let's go somewhere else. My stomach's rumbling; don't make me wait any longer."

"Come on, Giorgio, another ten minutes," I responded. "You'll see, something will open up." I didn't want to part with those eyes.

"Why are you so keen to stay here? Got your eye on some guy?"

I smiled and nodded.

He sighed and said, "We've had a long talk about this, Melissa. Chill out for a while; nice things happen by themselves."

"This time is different," I told him like a spoiled brat.

He sighed again and said they were going to check out other places in the neighbourhood. If they found a table, they'd grab it. I'd just have to follow.

"OK!" I said, certain they wouldn't find anything at that hour. I saw them go into the ice cream parlor with the Japanese umbrellas over the tables. Then I returned to the streetlight, trying as hard as possible not to look at him. All of a sudden, I saw him stand up. I think my face must have turned purple, I didn't know what to do, I was mortally embarrassed. So I turned toward the street and pretended I was waiting for someone, looking into all the cars that arrived. My Indian silk trousers fluttered in the light wind coming off the sea.

I heard his warm, deep voice at my back. He said, "What are you waiting for?"

Out of the blue I thought of an old rhyme I read as a child. It appeared in a fairy tale that my father had brought back from one of his trips. In a way that was spontaneous and unexpected, I recited it as I turned toward him:

> *I wait and wait till the sun goes down,*
> *and open the gate when someone comes round.*
> *After failure comes success,*
> *why this is so he'll never guess.*

We remained silent, our faces frozen; then we burst out laughing. He offered me a soft hand, and I squeezed it gently but with determination.

"Claudio," he said without removing his eyes from mine.

"Melissa." I don't know how I managed to get it out.

"What were you just saying?"

"What?... Oh, you mean the rhyme. It's from some fairy tale. I learned it by heart when I was seven."

He nodded as if to say he understood. Another panic-stricken silence. It was broken by my clumsy yet simpatico friend who had just run up, saying, "Come on, silly. We've found a table; we're waiting for you."

"I have to go," I murmured.

"May I knock at your gate?" He too spoke softly.

I looked at him, amazed at his boldness. He wasn't being cocky; he just didn't want everything to end there.

I nodded, my eyes teary, and said, "You can easily find me in the neighbourhood. Actually, that's my room up there." I pointed to my balcony.

"Then I'll come and serenade you," he said with a wink.

We said goodbye, and I didn't turn around to look at him one more time, as I would've liked: I was afraid of ruining everything.

Giorgio asked me, "Who was that?"

I smiled and said, "Someone who'll never guess."

"Hunh?" was his response.

I smiled again, pinched his cheek, and said, "You'll find out soon enough. Chill!"

4 June 2002
6:20 pm

He wasn't joking, Diary! He really did come to serenade me! People stopped to watch, burning with curiosity, and I was laughing on the balcony like a lunatic. A portly, red-faced man played a battered guitar, and the prince sang like sweet bells, jangled, out of tune, yet irresistible. Irresistible the way the song filled my eyes and heart. It was an old Sicilian song about a man who was left sleepless by thoughts of his beloved. The melody was at once delicate and agonizing. It went more or less like this:

> *I toss and turn and can't stop sighing,*
> *Every night I spend awake.*
> *Your beauty has me analyzing,*
> *I think of you without a break.*
> *For you I gave up my reprieve,*
> *This tortured heart can find no peace.*
> *It begs to know when you I'll leave –*
> *When my life ends and I surcease.*

It was a grand gesture, a shrewd courtship, traditional, some might even say banal, but nonetheless full of charm.

When he had finished, I said jokingly from the balcony, "Now what should I do? If I'm not mistaken, I would need to signal my acceptance of your suit by switching on the light in my bedroom. If, however, I wish to refuse, I must go back inside and switch it off."

He didn't respond, but I understood what I had to do. In the hallway I ran into my father (I nearly knocked him down!). He wanted to know who that guy was singing in the street. I burst out laughing and answered that I hadn't slightest idea.

I dashed down the stairs, just as I was, in shorts and a pullover. Yet when I opened the door, I suddenly stopped in my tracks. Should I run up to him and give him a big hug or just smile and thank him with a handshake? I remained motionless in the doorway, and he realized I wouldn't approach him if I didn't have some sort of signal. So he gave me one.

"You look like a frightened chick. Forgive my intrusiveness, but I was overwhelmed."

He embraced me gently, while I kept my arms at my sides. I couldn't imitate his gesture.

"Melissa, would you allow me to invite you to supper this evening?"

I nodded my consent and smiled. Then I sweetly kissed his cheek and went back inside.

"Who was he?" my mother asked, intensely curious.

I shrugged. "Nobody, Mamma, nobody."

12:45 pm

We spoke about ourselves. We talked about more than I had expected to say and hear. He's twenty and studies modern literature. His face has an animated, intelligent look that makes him incredibly attractive. I listened to him attentively; I liked watching him speak. I feel a flutter in my throat, my stomach. I feel as if I were bent back upon myself, like the stem of a flower, although I haven't snapped yet. Claudio is gentle, calm, reassuring. He told me he has experienced love, but it slipped from his hands.

He ran a finger around the rim of his glass and asked,

"What about you? What can you tell me about yourself?"

I opened up. A tiny gleam of light tore through the dense fog that enveloped my soul. I told him a bit about me, about my unhappy affairs, but I did no more than glance at my desire to find and uncover true feeling.

He gazed at me with attentive, sad, serious eyes and said, "I'm glad you've told me about your past. It reinforces the idea I'd formed of you."

"What idea?" I asked, fearful that he might accuse me of being too easy.

"That you're a girl – excuse me, a woman – who has gone through certain situations to arrive at what she is, to assume an outlook and absorb it so deeply. Melissa, I've never met a woman like you. I've gone from feeling an affectionate tenderness to experiencing a mysterious, irresistible fascination." His conversation was broken by long silences, during which he offered me his eyes and then resumed.

I smiled and said, "You still don't know me well enough to say that. You couldn't possibly have experienced all the feelings you've mentioned – maybe one of them, or none."

"But it's true," he said after listening to me carefully. "I want to try to get to know you. Will you allow me?"

"Of course, I'll let you!" I said, grabbing his hand from the table.

I felt as if I were in a dream, Diary, a most beautiful, endless dream.

1:20 am

I just received a message from Valerio, who says he wants to see me. The thought of him has now receded into the distance. I know that all I need to do is make love with the Prof one last time to be sure of what I really want and what

Melissa really is, whether a monster or someone who is truly capable of giving and receiving love.

10 June 2002

Fabulous: school is over! This year the results have been rather disappointing, I didn't apply myself very much, and my teachers didn't make an effort to understand me. Nonetheless, I did merit promotion. They stopped short of destroying me for good.

This afternoon I saw Valerio. He asked me to meet him at Bar Epoca. I rushed to get there, thinking it would be an opportunity to find out what I really wanted. When I arrived, I slammed on the brakes and left skid marks on the asphalt, drawing everyone's attention. Valerio was sitting at a table by himself, watching me, smiling and shaking his head at my every movement. I tried to appear nonchalant, walking slowly and assuming a serious expression.

I headed toward his table, swaying my hips, and when I got close to him, he told me, "Lo, didn't you see how everyone looked at you as you walked over?"

I shook my head no.

"I rarely pay attention to the looks."

A man came up behind Valerio. He had a mysterious, somewhat crusty air. He introduced himself to me, saying his name was Flavio. I scrutinized him carefully, but he cut off my investigation by remarking, "Your girl's eyes are too beautiful and too sly for someone her age."

I didn't let Valerio respond. "You're right, Flavio. So, are we going to be a threesome or will others join us?" I cut to the chase, Diary. I can't bother with smiles and pleasantries when there's only one item on the agenda.

Slightly embarrassed, Flavio looked at Valerio and said,

"She's skittish, but you should listen to what she says."

"Look, Melissa," Flavio continued, "Valerio and I intended to include you in a particular kind of soirée. He told me about you. I was a bit taken aback by your age, but after seeing what you're like . . . well, I've given in, and I'm curious to see you in action."

I said simply, "How old are you, Flavio?"

He said he was thirty-five. I nodded. I thought he might have been older, but I believed him.

"When is this particular soirée?" I asked.

"Next Saturday, at 10 pm, in a villa by the sea. I'll come to fetch you . . . with Valerio, of course, and—"

"If I should agree," I interrupted him.

"Certainly, if you should agree."

A few seconds of silence. Then I asked, "Do I have to wear something special?"

"It's best if your age isn't too noticeable," answered Flavio. "Everyone thinks you're eighteen."

"Everyone? How many are there?" I asked, turning towards Valerio.

"We don't know the exact number. Five couples for sure. Other people may show up, but at this point we can't say."

I decided to participate. I feel sorry for Claudio, but I'm not certain someone like me is capable of loving him. And I don't believe I can make him happy.

15 June 2002

No, I'm not the girl who can make him happy. I don't deserve him. My phone keeps ringing with his calls and messages. And here I am, dropping him. I'm not answering, I'm ignoring him altogether. He'll get fed up and look for happiness elsewhere. So why this fear?

17 June 2002

In silence, amid sporadic chitchat, we headed for the place that had been arranged for the gathering. It was a villa outside the city, on a part of the coast where the rocks break up and turn into sand. The place was deserted, the house set back from the road. We entered through a tall iron gate. I counted the parked cars: there were six of them.

"We've arrived, sweatheart." Flavio really rubs me the wrong way with these terms of endearment. Who the hell does he think he is? How can he allow himself to call me sweatheart, darling, little one? I'll strangle him!

The door was opened by a forty-something woman, attractive and perfumed. She looked me up and down and gave an approving glance to Flavio, who smiled faintly. We walked down a long hallway whose walls were hung with large abstract paintings. When we reached the living room, I felt deeply embarrassed: ten pairs of eyes suddenly fastened on me. Most of them belonged to distinguished-looking men who sported ties. Someone was wearing a mask that covered his face, but the others were barefaced. A few women drew near and asked me questions to which I responded with a series of lies rehearsed beforehand with Valerio. The Prof came to my side and whispered, "I can't wait to begin. I want to lick you, stay inside you all night, and then watch while you do it with the others."

I immediately thought of Claudio's smile: he would never desire to see me in bed with someone else.

Flavio brought me a glass of cream liqueur. It brought to mind that night last December. I went to the piano to think about how I'd got rid of Roberto a few days ago. I threatened to tell his girlfriend everything if he didn't stop calling me and didn't tell his friends to keep their mouths shut about me. It worked: I haven't heard a peep out of him!

At a certain point, a man of about thirty came toward me, walking with such a light step he seemed to be flying. He wore a pair of round glasses. His huge eyes were blue-green, his face pockmarked but handsome.

He scrutinized me carefully, then said, "*Ciao.* You're the one I've heard so much about?"

I gave him a questioning look and replied, "It depends on whom you have in mind. What exactly have you heard?"

"Well, we know you're very young, even if I personally don't believe you're eighteen yet. And not because you don't look it, but because I feel it. Anyhow, they told me you've participated in soirées like this on many occasions, although only with men."

I blushed and wanted to sink. "Who told you this?"

"Bah, what does it matter? People talk . . . You're a pretty little slut, aren't you?" He smiled.

I tried to stay calm and play the game without ruining everything.

"I've never been into planned encounters. I agreed to do it because I wanted to."

He stared at me, knowing full well that I was lying. Still, he went along with it. "There are always plans of one sort or another. Some people have plans that are linear and orderly, while others prefer a more rococo caprice."

"And then there's mine: a bit of both," I said, fascinated by his response.

Valerio approached and told me to join him on the sofa.

I nodded to the man, although I didn't say goodbye since I was almost certain that during the soirée we would wind up penetrating each other.

Sitting on the sofa was a muscular young man and two vulgar women wearing heavy makeup, garish and provocative. One had platinum blond hair.

The Prof and I sat in the centre of this huge sofa. With one hand he began to caress my breast beneath my pullover, immediately dragging me through shame and embarrassment.

"Come on, Valerio, do we really have to be the ones to start?"

"Why not? Don't you like it?" he asked, biting my earlobe.

"I was thinking just the opposite," The muscular one brashly remarked. "She has desire written all over her face."

"Desire for what?" I said defiantly.

He didn't respond. Instead he shot a hand beneath my skirt and worked it between my thighs, kissing me furiously. I was beginning to let myself go, but his silly violence was dragging me away again. I lifted my buttocks a bit to kiss him, and the Prof took advantage of this move. He caressed my ass with slow, gentle gestures that gradually turned hot and determined. The people around me no longer existed, even if they were there, watching me, waiting for one of the two men to penetrate me. While Muscles was kissing me, one of the women snaked her arms around his chest and kissed his neck. Then Valerio lifted my skirt: everyone was admiring my ass and my sex, flaunted on a strange sofa amongst strangers. My back was arched, and I was offering myself completely to him while Muscles was grabbing my tits and squeezing them hard.

"Mmmm, you're as fragrant as a young peach," said a man who had come up to nuzzle me, "soft and smooth, just washed, fresh."

The young peach will ripen, whereupon it will lose first its colour, then its taste, and then its skin will soften and sag. Finally, it will rot, and worms will suck out the pulp.

I opened my eyes wide; my face reddened. Suddenly I turned toward the Professor and said, "Let's go. I don't want this."

It happened just at the moment when my body was yielding completely... Poor Flavio, poor Muscles, poor

everybody, poor me. I abandoned them all, including my
hard–as–nails self. I got it together fast and, with tears in my
eyes, ran down the long hallway. I opened the door and
made for the car sitting in the road. Its windows were
fogged with the thick humidity that wrapped the house and
me.

Not a word on the way back. Only when I reached the
gate of my house did I tell him. "You still haven't said
anything about the letter."

A long silence, then simply, "Adieu, Lolita."

20 June
6:50 am

I put my lips to the phone and heard his voice scarcely
roused from sleep. "I want to live with you," I whispered, my
voice a thread.

24 June

Night has fallen, Diary, and I am on the terrace outside the
house, watching the sea.

It's so calm, quiet, pleasant; the tempered heat tones down
the waves, and I hear their roar in the distance, peaceful and
delicate . . . The moon is partly hidden; it seems to be
watching me with its compassionate, indulgent gaze.

I ask her what I should do.

It is difficult, she tells me, to strip away incrustations from
one's heart.

My heart . . . I don't recall having one. Perhaps I've never
known if I do.

A touching scene at the cinema never touched me, a powerful song never moved me, and I've always only half–believed in love, thinking I could never actually experience it. Yet I've never been cynical. No, the fact is that nobody ever taught me how to express the love I kept hidden inside, concealed from everyone. It was somewhere, it needed to be tracked down. I tried, flinging my desire into a world from which love was banished. And nobody, I mean nobody, blocked my path, saying, "No, little one, you can't enter here."

My heart was locked in a frozen cell. To break through it with a decisive blow would have been risky: my heart might have been shattered forever.

But then the sun arrived, not this Sicilian sun, which burns, inflames, belches fire, but a mild, discreet, generous sun, which melted the ice slowly and thus avoided any sudden flooding of my arid soul.

In the beginning, I felt I ought to ask him when we should make love, but later, when I was about to, I bit my lip. He realized something was up and asked me, "What is it, Melissa?" He calls me by my name; to him I am Melissa, I am a person, an essence, not an object, a body.

I shook my head. "Nothing, Claudio, really."

Then he took my hand and placed it on his chest.

I took a deep breath and stammered out, "I was asking myself when you'd want to make love."

He was silent, and I was mortified. I felt my cheeks burn.

"No, Melissa, love, I'm not the one who should decide when we'll make love. We'll decide together if and when we do it. It'll be you and me, together." He smiled.

I gazed at him, astonished, and he realized my stunned look begged him to continue.

"Because, you see, when two people join it is the height of spirituality, and this can be achieved only if they love each other. It's like a whirlpool enveloping their bodies, and they are no longer themselves. One is inside the other in the deepest, most intimate, and most beautiful way."

Even more amazed, I asked him what he meant.

He replied, "I'm in love with you, Melissa."

Why does this man believe so deeply in what I considered an impossibility only a few days ago? Why has life shown me nothing but wickedness, filth, and brutality till now? Can this extraordinary creature offer me a hand and raise me from the cramped, stinking hole where I crouch in fear? Moon, do you think he can do it?

Incrustations are hard to remove from one's heart. But perhaps this heart can beat strongly enough to shatter its carapace into a thousand pieces.

30 June

My ankles and wrists feel bound by an invisible rope. I'm suspended in the air and someone is pulling from below, shouting in a hellish voice, while someone else is pulling from above. I jerk up and down, weeping, sometimes touching clouds, sometimes worms. I keep repeating my name – Melissa, Melissa, Melissa – like some magic word that can save me. I grab hold of myself and cling to me.

7 July

I've repainted the walls of my room; now they're pale blue. Marlene Dietrich's languid gaze no longer looks over my desk; now there's a photo of me, my hair in the wind, as I calmly observe the chalk-stained boats in the port. Behind me stands Claudio, his arms encircling my waist, his hands resting delicately on my white blouse, lowering his face to plant a kiss on my shoulder. He seems not to notice the boats, but rather to be absorbed in contemplating us.

After the photo was snapped, he whispered in my ear, "Melissa, I love you."

I rested my cheek against his, breathed deeply to savour the moment, and turned around. I took his face in my hands and kissed him with a tenderness I never felt before. Then I whispered, "I love you too, Claudio."

A shiver, then a feverish heat ran through my body till I abandoned myself in his arms and he held me more tightly, kissing me with a passion that wasn't sexual desire, but a yearning for something else, for love.

I wept uncontrollably, wept as I had never done in front of someone.

"Please help me, my love," I implored.

"I am here for you," he said, holding me as no man has ever held me.

13 July

We fell asleep on the beach in a tight embrace, warmed by each other's arms. His integrity, his respect make me tremble with envy. Can I ever repay him for all this loveliness?

24 July

Fear, utter fear.

30 July

I run away, and he catches up with me. It's so sweet to feel his hands hold me without oppressing me. I weep often, and whenever I do, he holds me tight, his breath in my hair, and I rest my face against his chest. I am tempted to flee, to slide back into the abyss, to return to the tunnel and never leave it. But his arms support me and I trust them and I can still save myself...

12 August 2002

My desire for him is strong and intense; I can't do without his presence. He hugs me, asks me who I belong to.

"I'm yours," I answer, "completely yours."

He looks me in the eyes and tells me, "Little one, please don't hurt yourself. That would hurt me very much."

"I wouldn't ever hurt you," I tell him.

"You shouldn't do it for me, but for yourself, above all else. You're a flower; don't let them trample on you anymore."

He kisses me, softly grazing my lips, and fills me with love.

I smile, I'm happy. He tells me, "Look, now I have to kiss you, I have to steal this smile from you and print it forever on my lips. You drive me crazy, you're an angel, a princess, I want to devote an entire night to loving you."

In a pure white bed our bodies fit together perfectly. His skin joins with mine, and together we become strength and gentleness. We gaze into each other's eyes as he slowly slips inside me, without hurting, because he says my body mustn't be violated, just loved. I clasp him with my arms and legs, his sighs join with mine, his fingers intertwine with mine, and his pleasure blends inevitably with mine.

I fall asleep on his chest, my long hair covering his face, but he is happy about it and kisses me hundreds of times on the head. "Promise me one thing," I whisper to him, "promise me we'll never part."

Another silence. He caresses my back, and I feel irresistible shivers. He penetrates me again as I thrust my hips, sticking to his.

And while I move slowly, he says, "Whether we part depends on two conditions. You shouldn't feel imprisoned by me or my love, my affection, anything. You're an angel who must fly free; you should never allow me to be the sole purpose of your life. You're going to be a great woman, and now you know it."

In a voice broken with pleasure I ask him what is the second condition.

"Never betray yourself, because if you do you'll hurt both of us. I love you, and I will love you even if our paths should divide."

Our pleasures fuse. I can't help but hold my Love tightly and never ever leave him.

I fall asleep on his bed, spent. The night passes, and in the morning I am awakened by the hot, radiant sun. I find his note on the pillow:

May your life be filled with the highest, fullest, and most perfect happiness, marvellous creature. And may I play a part in it, as long as you would like. Because . . . from now on you must know: I would like it to be forever, even when you no longer turn around to look at me. I've gone to get you breakfast; I'll be back soon.

With one eye open I observe the sun. Soft sounds reach my ear. The fishermen's boats are beginning to dock after a night spent at sea. A journey into the unknown. A tear streams down my face. I smile when his hand grazes my bare back, and he kisses my neck. I look at him. I look at him and understand. Now I know.

I have concluded my journey in the forest, I have managed to escape from the ogre's tower, from the clutches of the tempting angel and his devils, I have run away from the androgynous monster. And I have ended up in the castle of the Arab prince, who was expecting me, seated on a soft velvet pillow. He had me strip off my threadbare clothes and gave me the garments of a princess. He summoned the maidservants and commanded them to brush my hair. Then he kissed me on the forehead and said that he would watch me while I slept. One night we made love, and when I returned home I saw that my hair was still shining and my makeup intact. A princess, as my mother always says, so beautiful that even dreams want to steal her away.